The Vampire Next Door

by

Marilyn Baron

A Psychic Crystal Mystery, Book 4

The Vampire Next Door

Cover Art by *Debbie Taylor*

The Wild Rose Press, Inc.
PO Box 708
Adams Basin, NY 14410-0708
Visit us at www.thewildrosepress.com

Publishing History
First Black Rose Edition, 2017
Print ISBN 978-1-5092-1490-7
Digital ISBN 978-1-5092-1491-4

A Psychic Crystal Mystery, Book 4
Published in the United States of America

Aurora Dawn threw open her bedroom window to welcome the sunlight and lowered her long blonde locks down the brick wall, Rapunzel-style, something she'd done every day since she was a teenager. What was she waiting for? Who was she waiting for? Yearning for? Prince Charming? Or just someone to rescue her from an arranged marriage that would ruin her life?

She listened for sounds emanating from the walled mansion next door. All she heard was the jarring sound of lawn machinery, buzzing through the thickets. There would be no last-minute reprieve.

For weeks, as the wedding got closer, Aurora Dawn's nerves had become more frayed. She had been hesitant to face the truth. And the truth was she didn't want to marry Bronx Bamberger. She was a coward. She couldn't confront her fiancé, and she was afraid to tell her mother. Her mother had been working tirelessly for a year with Bronx's mother, Betsey, to plan the perfect wedding. How could she disappoint her parents and bring all those expensive plans crashing down around her family? It would be a disgrace. It would be the topic for tabloids, and it wasn't fair to her mother, who hated publicity. She had gone along because she did love Bronx in a way. They had been best friends for years. But it wasn't the kind of love that stirred her heart, the passionate kind of love she knew was out there.

Then she saw a face staring out at her from the upstairs window across the yard. The new boy—no, a man really, judging from the sheer size of him. Her heart fluttered with a primal hunger.

Dedication

I dedicate this book to my husband, Steve,
for all his love and support
and for giving me the idea for this book.

Marilyn Baron's Contest Wins

The Colonoscopy Club (now the published novel *STONES*) finaled in the GRW Unpublished Maggie Awards for Excellence in 2005 in the Single Title category.

The Edger won first place in the Suspense Romance category of the 2010 Ignite the Flame Contest, sponsored by the Central Ohio Fiction Writers chapter of RWA.

SIXTH SENSE won the GRW 2012 Unpublished Maggie Award for Excellence in the Paranormal/Fantasy Romance category.

SIGNIFICANT OTHERS was a finalist in the 2014 GRW Published Maggie Awards for Excellence in the Novel With Strong Romantic Elements category.

Prologue

Gedeon's sinful soul split open like an overripe melon, and he didn't even know he had one. In his last lucid memory, he was manacled in silver handcuffs to the helm on the deck of a yacht moored in Bermuda at dawn. The searing light of the sun as it spilled over the horizon had damned near incinerated him. A final flash permeated his brain. A brief, agonizing, but illuminating vision of his long-lost love, Marika—a girl he had been promised to since childhood—flooded his mind.

Before he passed out, Gedeon harbored vague thoughts of revenge and taking back what was his, but he'd have to wait until he was stronger, much stronger. The blinding light had sapped his strength, zapped the core of his being. Then he was here, but where was here? Heaven? Hell? Purgatory?

Chapter One

Juliette Bradley shifted restlessly in her husband's arms. "Will, I'm uneasy. I feel an ominous presence. I feel an evil spirit. It's close. So close. It feels a lot like—"

Juliette's eyes widened and her breathing came in shallow waves. Will knew never to underestimate his wife or discount her feelings. She was rarely wrong about anything. He kissed Juliette on the forehead and snapped on the crystal table lamp. His first thought was to get his hands on his gun in the drawer, even though a gun was useless against a being such as he had encountered that night in Bermuda, unless it was loaded with silver bullets.

He was distracted when Juliette's purple silk nightgown slipped off one shoulder, revealing a hint of pale breast illuminated by the moonlight. He touched her naked shoulder, and she shivered.

"Still having those nightmares, honey? You know Jack and I destroyed Gedeon Nagy more than twenty years ago on the yacht in Bermuda. I saw it happen. There was nothing left of whoever or whatever it was. He can't hurt you anymore."

"I know what you saw, but I also know how I feel." Juliette looked out the window. "It's a full moon. In the morning, I'll put another protective spell on Aurora Dawn before her wedding celebration."

"Aurora Dawn is a strong woman. She's your granddaughter, after all. Her power is growing exponentially. You've taught her well."

"I know, but she is precious above all else to me, and I would see her protected."

"She has your amulet."

"But I can do more. I must do more."

"Bronx will protect her. He'll be by her side forever."

"Forever is a relative term," Juliette reminded him. "And he may be a handsome devil, but Bronx Bamberger is also a pompous ass, just like his father. I can't fathom what Aurora Dawn sees in him. Kate rejected his father's marriage proposal, but now the Bambergers are finally getting their hooks into the Crystal fortune and my granddaughter's power."

"The Bambergers don't need Aurora Dawn's money. They're already richer than God."

"But it's never enough for them."

"You don't really think Bronx has evil intentions toward Aurora Dawn, do you? He's in love with her. Always has been, since they were children."

"It's not Bronx I'm worried about. It's someone from the past, *my* past."

"Should we warn Kate and Jack?"

"I hate to worry them. My daughter has her hands full, with the wedding only a week away, but I'll have a talk with her this morning."

"It's still dark out. Why don't you go back to sleep?"

"I can't."

"What can I do to help?"

Juliette sighed. "Just hold me, Will."

"I can do better than that." Will turned off the light, took Juliette in his arms, and pressed his lips against hers.

"You can always make me forget, Will Bradley."

Will would never forget what had happened twenty-four years ago, and he doubted his son-in-law Jack would, either. He deepened the kiss, reminding himself to check his weapon as soon as he got out of bed. And reminding himself, for the umpteenth time, that there were no such things as vampires.

Chapter Two

Jack Hale looked out the bedroom window through the slats in the white plantation shutters. "Kate, did you notice that the For Sale sign is finally down on the monstrosity next door?"

Sitting at the dressing table, getting ready for bed, Katherine Crystal Hale fingered the strand of pearls Jack had given her on their wedding day. The pearls she would present to her daughter, Aurora Dawn, before she walked down the aisle right here in her family home in one week. "You mean the Stryer mansion?"

"Yes. That house has more turrets than Hogwarts Castle. And it's so overgrown with trees and brambles and thorns, it's going to take a lawn crew months to clear it out."

"Unfortunately, it won't happen in time for the wedding. That house is a blight on the neighborhood. I'm glad we're going to have new neighbors. Aurora Dawn is going to be so excited. She's always thought an enchantress must have cast a spell over that house, like in Sleeping Beauty, and that one day her Prince Charming was going to materialize out of the forest. She's been waiting for him ever since."

"Isn't Bronx her Prince Charming?"

"You'd think so. But I think she's dreaming of more, of a knight in shining armor astride a white steed, to rescue her."

"Rescue her from what? The life of being a pampered heiress?"

"I think she wants to be more than that. I know you were hoping she could take Will's place in the business when he retires. But she wants to be a writer. She writes stories about dragons and witches, vampires rising, and werewolves howling in darkened cemeteries, because my mother has been feeding her a steady diet of fairy tales since she was born. That's why her head is always in the clouds. She has quite an imagination."

"Vampires are not exactly literary fiction, Kate. Doesn't she want to be a serious writer?"

"Vampires are trending, darling. It's called paranormal. And it's all the rage. She studied creative writing in college. She thinks she can make a living at it."

"Don't tell Bronx that. He imagines her as the perfect society wife. No wife of his is going to work. And he's right. Why does she need to make a living? She will never have to work a day in her life if she doesn't want to."

"Jack. Do you hear what you're saying? I didn't choose that kind of life for myself, so why should I want that for my daughter? My life is full of scary characters too—serial killers and various and sundry murderers. Only those characters aren't mythical. They actually exist. Don't you think what we do for a living might have influenced her?"

Jack frowned. "I guess we're lucky she doesn't want to be a psychic like you and her grandmother, or a Romani like her great-grandmother. And who in their right mind would paint a house fuchsia?"

"You're changing the subject, and you know

fuchsia is my mother's favorite color. She's always loved that house next door. She wanted me to get ours repainted, but I had to draw the line."

"Maybe I should have said, who but an eccentric psychic would paint her house purple?"

"That house next door is an authentic Neel Reid, built in the 1920s," Kate noted. "Even if it is haunted. People would kill for a house like that."

"In fact, people *have* killed in that house," Jack agreed. "That's why it's been on the market for so long, no matter what color they paint it or how much they lower the price, they can't paper over what took place there. How do you know it's haunted?"

"Everyone in the neighborhood knows," Kate said. "But that bloodbath was a long time ago."

"They never caught the killers. The police think it was some kind of a death cult, but the perpetrators just disappeared into thin air. It was a Manson-style murder, and you can never wipe off the stain of gruesome death."

Kate shuddered. "I still have nightmares about it. My adoptive parents were alive then. I was just a little girl at the time. It could have been me and my family. We were just one house over. That was the first time I realized I had psychic abilities. I woke my mother up in the middle of the night and insisted there was something wrong next door. I heard pleas, a woman begging for mercy, followed by screams. Horrible screams. In my head. No one else could hear them."

"What did your mother do when you told her?"

Kate frowned. "She put me back to bed and told me to go to sleep. And then when we found out the next day what had happened, she told me to keep quiet and never mention it again. They were afraid of my visions, the voices in my head, the premonitions. They didn't understand me."

"Maybe I should get the police to reopen the cold case, or at least investigate," Jack offered.

"Darling, it's not necessary to vet our new neighbors. If they can afford to live there, they're probably okay."

"So you think there can't be wealthy serial killers? I've seen all kinds in my business. Besides, we can't be too careful. We have a child in the house."

Kate laughed. "That child, as you call her, is about to become a bride, and she'll be moving out soon."

"All right, a child bride, but I've got to protect my family." Jack peered out the window at the house on the hill next door. "Why don't you and your mother go over there and introduce yourselves tomorrow morning? See if you get any of your *woo-woo* feelings."

"I thought you didn't like it when I practiced 'witchcraft,' as you call it, except when I'm helping you solve your cases. Then I'm a gifted psychic."

"You could borrow a cup of sugar," Jack suggested.

Kate placed the pearls gingerly on the mirrored surface. "That's so Donna Reed. And besides, they probably have an alarm system, or they should, with the rash of robberies we've been having in this neighborhood. I'm sure they know nothing about the murders that took place in their house. Although isn't it the responsibility of the realtor to disclose that?

"I saw a black stretch limousine with tinted windows crawling up their driveway earlier this evening," Kate observed, turning in the direction of the house next door. "It was in and out of the garage at all hours of the evening, under cover of darkness. There's a lot of activity over there. I heard it was a mother, father, and son who moved in. The realtor mentioned something about a blended family. What does that mean? A family of vampires and shifters? And the deer population in the neighborhood is thinning. That's a bad sign. They seem to have an unusual amount of trash for a family of three. Don't you think that's strange? I wonder what they're hiding?"

"Probably typical for a family that's just moved in," Jack concluded. "And what makes you think they're hiding something? I believe you're overthinking this. Aurora Dawn inherited her vivid imagination from her mother. And who knows? Maybe they're movie stars trying to take a break from the spotlight. Some people might think we're strange, too, *Crystal Ball Kate,* living in the Crystal Palace. We may as well live in a fishbowl."

Kate pursed her lips. She thought she had outgrown that moniker. Thought she'd left those headlines behind. *Atlanta Socialite Katherine Crystal Inherits Her Murdered Parents' Fortune; Seer to the Stars Helps Solve High Profile Serial Killer Cases*. Hoped all that business about her sociopath birth father was long forgotten. But there were parts of the story she didn't want to forget. She had found her birth mother, Juliette, then too, when she and Jack investigated the mystery surrounding her own birth, after her parents were killed in a suspicious car crash.

All this talk of murders dredged up the past, and she shook her head to clear her mind of the unwelcome thoughts.

Kate still worked with her mother and her husband, former Atlanta cop Jack Hale, who now ran the Crystal & Hale Psychic Detective Agency with her birth mother's husband, Will Bradley, a former small-town Florida sheriff. But Will was about to retire, and the heavy workload was falling on her husband's shoulders. She wasn't much help, since she spent virtually every moment planning Aurora Dawn's wedding.

Of course, her daughter's wedding would be the social event of the season, and the headlines were bound to reappear, opening the floodgates to all those unwanted memories, the nightmares of the past. Kate had experienced enough notoriety to last a lifetime. It had been good for their business, but after the birth of her daughter, Aurora Dawn, who had inherited the psychic powers of her mother, grandmother, and great-grandmother, she wanted to protect her daughter at any cost. Protect her from whoever was moving in next door. "I'm going to forbid Aurora Dawn from going over there."

Jack walked over to where Kate was seated and massaged her shoulders. "Forbid her? That never worked for you. She's too high spirited. And she's *your* daughter. Why not just tell her the house is haunted?"

"She already knows it," Kate insisted. "That just makes the new neighbors more intriguing. Anyway, there's something weird about the new people. They never show themselves during the day."

Jack laughed. "You think we're living next to a family of vampires—the undead?"

"Well, no," Kate admitted. "That would be ridiculous, wouldn't it?"

"I still have a lot of contacts in law enforcement.

I'll check them out, if it will make you feel better."

"I think that would be wise, Jack. And I'm getting a bad feeling about those people. I think evil has moved in next door."

"Evil?"

"You don't believe me?"

"Kate, sweetheart, I learned a long time ago never to doubt you."

Kate shivered involuntarily. "I'm afraid our past has come back to haunt us."

Jack gathered Kate in his arms. "Don't be afraid. Everything will be okay. I'll make sure of it."

****

Kate had tossed and turned, and when she was finally asleep, Jack put on a comfortable pair of jeans and a T-shirt and went downstairs. He doubted he would ever get used to living in such grand style, in the ritziest part of Atlanta, in a mansion everyone knew as the Crystal Palace. In the darkness, he bumped into someone entering the library.

He caught the man and wrestled him to the ground.

"Take it easy on the old man."

"Will? You scared me to death. What are you doing down here in the middle of the night?"

"Juliette was restless, and I couldn't sleep."

Jack gave Will a hand up. Will and Juliette occupied a wing on the other side of the house. But it wasn't Will's style to roam around the mansion at night. The place was big enough for both couples, and they respected each other's space and privacy.

"It was something Juliette said that got me nervous. I wanted to check it out."

The two men, in-laws and longtime business

partners, eyed each other. Neither had a psychic bone in their body, but they communicated the unspoken, nonetheless. They had experienced the unspeakable together.

Jack and Will entered the library, and Jack opened the safe. In there, he kept important papers and documents he hoped Kate would never have to see. He brought out a diary, a diary he and Will had read twenty-four years ago, a diary they had tried to forget about until this morning. When Kate and Juliette got their premonitions, they knew to take them seriously. Kate and her mother were seldom wrong. He and Will sat at the desk and began rereading the *Chronicles of Gedeon Nagy*.

After several hours, Jack put down the yellowed transcripts of the diary and rubbed his eyes. He and Will had killed Gedeon. Baked him alive on the boat in Bermuda.

"If Gedeon is still living and breathing in this world, in whatever form, he'll never give up trying to find her," Will lamented. "I'll have to keep a close watch on Juliette, the woman the monster thought was his long-lost Marika."

"And we'll have to keep tabs on Kate, and Aurora Dawn also," added Jack. "I hoped to God we were rid of that beast forever, whatever he was."

It had been more than twenty years with no sign that Gedeon had been resurrected. Nevertheless, Jack was spooked every time he passed the cemetery around the corner from the Crystal Palace in Buckhead. Did vampires rise from the dead? He had no idea, but he wasn't taking any chances with the centuries-old monster. And Jack didn't believe in vampires. But it wouldn't hurt to take precautions. He would protect his family to the death, if it came to that.

Chapter Three

Aurora Dawn threw open her bedroom window to welcome the sunlight and lowered her long blonde locks down the brick wall, Rapunzel-style, something she'd done every day since she was a teenager. What was she waiting for? Who was she waiting for? Yearning for? Prince Charming? Or just someone to rescue her from an arranged marriage that would ruin her life?

She listened for sounds emanating from the walled mansion next door. All she heard was the jarring sound of lawn machinery, buzzing through the thickets. There would be no last-minute reprieve.

For weeks, as the wedding got closer, Aurora Dawn's nerves had become more frayed. She had been hesitant to face the truth. And the truth was she didn't want to marry Bronx Bamberger. She was a coward. She couldn't confront her fiancé, and she was afraid to tell her mother. Her mother had been working tirelessly for a year with Bronx's mother, Betsey, to plan the perfect wedding. How could she disappoint her parents and bring all those expensive plans crashing down around her family? It would be a disgrace. It would be the topic for tabloids, and it wasn't fair to her mother, who hated publicity. She had gone along because she did love Bronx in a way. They had been best friends for years. But it wasn't the kind of love that stirred her heart, the passionate kind of love she knew was out there.

Then she saw a face staring out at her from the upstairs window across the yard. The new boy—no, a man really, judging from the sheer size of him. Her heart fluttered with a primal hunger. Her blood pulsed, and her spirit soared. When he took aim at her with his smile, something unexpected slammed into her chest with the blunt force of a bullet, speeding her heart rate with the piercing accuracy of Cupid's arrow. Now this...*this* was what she'd been waiting for. The man waved, and she beamed back. He signaled he would meet her downstairs. They were of the same mind, then. She nodded eagerly. She'd been a good, obedient girl her whole life. *And now she wanted to take a bite out of the boy next door.*

The thing about having a mother and grandmother who are powerful psychics is that they can tell if you're up to no good. And when they start weaving their protective spells around you, independently or collectively, there isn't much wiggle room to misbehave. You'd think they would check with each other before they did their casting, so they didn't overcompensate. Together, they were so powerful she was liable to end up in a Sleeping Beauty trance, in a castle like the one next door, surrounded by thick rose hedges and nasty thorns, hidden away from the world until she was awakened by a kiss. A kiss from her prince that released her from her spell. The forest surrounding the house next door was in dire need of thinning. And she was in dire need of—

Her mother and grandmother claimed she was a psychic superpower in her own right, but you'd hardly know it, Aurora Dawn thought, rushing down the stairs. She hadn't had the opportunity to stretch her wings. And these women weren't above stooping to cheap parlor tricks—levitations, contacting the dead, and such, which could be quite amusing for them, but rather embarrassing for her. In a family of psychics, there's absolutely no privacy. Between hearing other people's voices swirling around in her head and entertaining rebellious thoughts of her own, it often got pretty crowded in there.

Mom knew what was going to happen before it happened. Take the telephone, for instance. There was no need for Caller ID in the Hale household.

"Honey, get the phone, it's Margaret," her mother would say. And it always would be. Or "Honey, don't answer that, it's just a sales call." And it always was.

And try growing up in a neighborhood where people are convinced you're living with a coven of witches, which wasn't far from the truth. Not to mention that her father and grandfather had been cops and were now in the private investigation business, handling mostly high-profile murder and kidnapping cases. And that both kept a collection of guns in the house. It was a recipe to ensure that she never made a mistake, or even a misstep, or ever met a man who wasn't the safe son of her parents' best friends.

Naturally, being the new "it" girl, the daughter of the darling of Atlanta high society, she was engaged to the perfect guy—Bronx Bamberger—who happened to be the son of her mother's former fiancé, Justin Bamberger. Justin and Kate had grown up together and had been engaged briefly, but she'd broken it off and married Aurora Dawn's father. Mom found Bronx's dad to be an egomaniacal prig, so why was she subjecting her own daughter to a lifetime of certain boredom where banal bank talk would be the topic of the day at the breakfast table and corporate mergers probably the only talk in the bedroom?

Because Bronx Bamberger presented the perfect picture to the world. Perfect on paper. He was reasonably tall, dark, and handsome in every sense of the cliché, and smart and smooth (too smooth for her taste), rich and ruthless. He was looking for a malleable society wife, and she definitely did not fit the bill. She didn't know what she wanted to be yet, and she wasn't ready to lose her identity for a long-term commitment. But Bronx had been so relentless in his pursuit she'd grown weary and exhausted and, yes, flattered, so she'd finally relented and consented to marry him so she could get some peace.

Not that the wedding planning had allowed her any downtime. There were so many decisions to be made and plans to be approved. What to wear, what to serve, how to decorate, where to live... The wedding would be at the Crystal Palace, of course. Her parents' home was the perfect fairytale setting, courtesy of the best decorators money could buy. The Crystal Palace was right around the corner from the Bamberger estate. And Bronx had already picked out another mansion in their Buckhead neighborhood for their new home. Which meant she would be living practically next door to the home where she'd spent her entire life. Bronx had arranged everything and, if that was any indication, he had every intention of arranging the rest of her life.

Living in the Crystal Palace, not exactly your average Buckhead mansion, was bad enough without having to exist under a microscope. Which is why she was the only one of her friends who hadn't lost her virginity, and she was getting married in less than a week, hardly optimum. But she had a strong feeling her life was about to change in a big way as she rushed outside to meet her destiny.

She focused her violet eyes on the stranger standing at the bottom of her driveway and batted her eyelashes as she approached, while awareness of the man assaulted her like a body slam. Her feelings intensified as she got closer to him. This was the kind of attraction she had only read about in fairy tales and romance novels, had dreamt about as she tossed and turned restlessly in her bed. Her Prince Charming had come, and she was anxious to greet him.

"Hi, neighbor," said Aurora Dawn, grasping his hand to stop hers from shaking.

****

Aurora Dawn took his hand and the sun brightened. It was the first time in centuries that he'd been outside during daylight hours. It gave him a heady feeling, or maybe he was undone by the girl's beauty and her presence and her tinkling voice and the scorching touch of her hand. He had a sudden urge to reach out and run his fingers through her blonde locks. He'd seen her as a vision in the mirror, held by his Maker to tempt him, but he wasn't prepared for the reality of her.

"Hello, R-Rapunzel," he stuttered.

Aurora Dawn blushed. "That's not my name."

"Goldilocks, then. Your hair must have been spun from gold."

"That's Rumpelstiltskin, silly. I'm not the miller's daughter, and I don't live in a dungeon."

He looked up at her house. "No, you certainly do not."

She glanced up at his house in return. "And neither do you, it seems. What's your name?"

He hesitated before responding. "It's Lancelot. Lancelot Lakeland."

"Seriously? Like Lancelot of the Lake in King Arthur's court?"

"Yes, but you can call me Lance."

"Like a real live knight in shining armor?"

Lance shrugged. "And your name?" As if he didn't already know every single thing about her, hadn't been studying her for two decades, wasn't already in love with her.

"Aurora Dawn Hale."

"Because the sun rises and sets in your violet eyes?"

Aurora Dawn smiled, and his heart simmered.

That dazzling smile would be his undoing. What if he couldn't control his impulses and inadvertently took a bite out of Aurora Dawn Hale? Did he still have the capacity to turn her? Was his semi-vampiric state reversible? Did he even want it to be?

She reached up and pressed her thumb over the place where Lance's eyebrow should have been. Rubbed it back and forth until he almost dissolved with lust.

"What happened to your other eyebrow?"

Lance's hand flew to hers.

"Singed by a fire-breathing dragon."

Aurora Dawn laughed. "Will it ever grow back?"

"They say no. Does it disturb you?"

"I think it's sexy, like a battle scar."

Lance grunted. "There's a lot of activity at your house," he remarked as cars and vans pulled in and out of the driveway.

Aurora Dawn shrugged. "Just deliveries."

"For what?"

Aurora Dawn chewed thoughtfully on her bottom lip while Lance swung her hand back and forth.

"A wedding."

Lance brushed a lock of jet-black hair out of his eyes with his free hand and cocked his single eyebrow.

If he asked for specifics, she wouldn't be ready to give them, yet. She obviously found her new next-door neighbor far too interesting and tempting. The less he knew about her impending nuptials, the better, for now.

"Say, Aurora Dawn Hale, who do I have to slay around here to get a date?"

"Slay? Isn't that overkill?"

"It's just a figure of speech, a little dragon humor."

"Oh. Well, um, what did you have in mind? I'm pretty tied up most of this week."

"Tied up?" He smiled, all sorts of X-rated images dancing in his imagination. But that was his old persona, his bad persona. In his new incarnation, his thoughts were pure.

"Yes, but I'm open today."

Lance growled and tightened the reins on his emotions and his lascivious former self.

Lance knew she was playing with fire. Just five days away from her wedding, she had no business going out on a date with anyone, even if he was just the boy next door.

"I could show you the neighborhood," she suggested. "Then we could grab a bite."

Lance smiled. "A bite sounds perfect. I haven't eaten in…well, in a while. I've built up quite an appetite."

"Let me just grab my purse and tell my mother I'm going out."

"You still check in with your mother?"

"I live here, don't I? Anyway, it's just a courtesy. My mother knows what I'm planning before I do. In fact, I might ask her for some restaurant recommendations, since she probably already knows where I'm going to take you."

"Is she a mind reader?"

"She's more than that. She's a psychic. Haven't you ever heard of Crystal Ball Kate?"

Lance shook his head. He couldn't exactly be honest with her, so he avoided the question. "I'm new in the neighborhood."

"Are you new on the planet? My mother is a world-famous crime solver. She works with my dad in their psychic detective agency. There's nothing that woman doesn't know. And what she doesn't know, my dad can find out. He's a great tracker. So is Grandpa. He used to be a sheriff in Florida. And my grandmother is an even more talented psychic than my mother."

Lance frowned. Tangling with law enforcement and psychics was the last thing he wanted to do. Especially the people in the psychic viper's nest who lived next door. He intended to remain under the radar. His plan to woo and win Aurora Dawn depended on it.

He released his hold on her hand. "I'll just run up and get my car and meet you back down at the bottom of the driveway."

When Aurora Dawn turned and headed to her

house, Lance made an instinctive attempt to fly back up the driveway to get his car, he was that anxious, but it all fell apart. He'd forgotten. He couldn't fly anymore. He *could* walk in the sunlight. And he *could* eat human food. And he *could* breathe in the fresh scent of his new love. A day of firsts. Something to be grateful for on this first day of the rest of his life.

Chapter Four

"Mom, I'm going out," Aurora Dawn called up to her mother.

Kate bounded down the staircase. "Wait a minute, honey. You have your final dress fitting today, remember? We need to be at the dress shop by three o'clock."

"I didn't forget. But I'm—"

"I saw you talking to the boy next door," Kate said, her tone hinting of disapproval, the toe of her fashionable black ballet slipper tapping against the marble floor.

Aurora Dawn rolled her eyes. "I figured you did, and you didn't ask where I was going, so tell me, where *am* I going?"

"I hope nowhere. That's what I want to talk to you about. We don't know anything about these people who moved in next door. For all we know, they could be serial killers."

"Mom, you're kidding, right? I think you've been working with Dad too long."

"No, actually, I'm serious. I have a bad feeling about that boy. So does your grandmother. She thinks he might be dangerous."

"Mom, have you seen him? He's dangerously gorgeous."

"Not up close, but I am getting a bad reading. I can

sense evil. I mean, you can too, can't you? And bad things often come in pretty packages. Things that aren't good for us."

"Mom, can I ask you a question?"

Kate nodded.

"When you first met Dad, could you read him? I mean could you tell what he was thinking?"

Kate laughed. "When I first saw your father, I thought he was the biggest jerk I'd ever met. He thought I was a fake and a publicity seeker. As a matter of fact, he called me a 'psycho broad.' We got off on the wrong foot right away. I was too mad to read him and then, well, after we worked together on a case, I fell madly, impossibly in love with him, and I was permanently blocked. In fact, when I look at your father, I can hardly see straight. Even after all these years."

"Remember you once told me that you couldn't read a man if you were truly in love with him? And that's true of Grandma Juliette. She can't read Grandpa. Well, I can read Bronx Bamberger like a bad novel. I can sense every thought that runs through his head. Always could. His mind is as porous as a sieve."

"Well, I'm sure there are exceptions to the rule. You've known Bronx since you two were in diapers. Maybe it's not a matter of being able to size him up as a psychic, but rather that you're such good friends, you're of the same mind, and can read each other's thoughts."

"Well, that's just it, Mom. Bronx and I are *friends* and of course I love him, but I'm not sure I'm *in love* with him."

"Aurora Dawn, why didn't you say anything about this to me before?"

"Well, I mean, you and the Bambergers are so close, and everyone was so happy about the wedding, and I know Bronx is chomping at the bit to get into my pants—"

"Aurora Dawn!"

"It's true. I've been fending him off for years, but for him, I think it's more about the chase and wanting what he can't have than true love. And when I look at him, I don't melt or anything. My heart doesn't... I mean, when I saw Lance, that's the boy next door, I thought I was going to burn up right there on the driveway."

"Well, it *is* hot outside."

"Mom, that's not what I mean."

"Exactly, what do you mean?"

"Maybe it's just lust, but it just hit me and I couldn't look away. Only it's more than that. I can't explain it. I'm drawn to him. And I can't stop thinking about him. And I can't wait to see him again."

"It's just a case of wanting to sow your wild oats before the wedding."

"That's just it. I haven't sown any wild oats with anyone but Bronx because he's always been there, and if I bring home anyone else, my family scares him away."

"We certainly didn't mean to do that."

"Dad has interrogated and investigated every one of my potential boyfriends."

"Well, he's very protective."

"You were engaged to Bronx's dad, and you were under pressure to marry him, but you married Dad instead. You married the man you loved. Why can't I?"

"Aurora Dawn, the wedding is five days away.

Guests are flying in from around the world. Everything is arranged. We can't call it off at this late date. It's just nerves."

"That's what I thought. And I don't want to cause problems, but I just want, for once, to do what *I* want to do and not what you or Daddy expect me to do."

"But Bronx Bamberger is a nice boy."

"Cats are nice. Dogs are nice. Babies are nice. And maybe I will be happy with Bronx, but don't I owe it to myself to find out for sure if there might be somebody else, something else out there for me?"

Kate blew out a breath. "I need to talk to your father."

"You mean you need to put Lance under a microscope. Well, go ahead then. His name is Lancelot Lakeland. That's all I know about him. That's all I need to know."

"Lancelot? Like Lancelot of the Lake? What kind of name is that?"

"A cool one. Now, I'm going to be neighborly and show our scrumptious new neighbor around and take him to lunch."

"How about Flip Burger Boutique on Howell Mill? That's good, and it's fast."

"Thanks, Mom. And don't worry. Nothing is going to happen."

Aurora Dawn skipped out the door and down the driveway so mad with desire she was afraid she'd disintegrate.

"Nice wheels," Aurora Dawn said as she slipped into the passenger seat of Lance's late-model blue Mercedes-Benz E-Class Cabriolet.

"I thought we'd ride with the top down. It's such a

beautiful day."

"I'd love that. First I'll show you around the neighborhood, and then we'll go to lunch. Where did you move from?"

"Hungary," Lance said.

"Can you speak any foreign languages?"

"A number of them." He rattled off a few: "French, Italian, Hungarian, of course, and German."

"Impressive. What kind of work do you do?"

Lance hesitated. "Import, export, mostly I deal in artwork."

"Well, then you would get along great with my mother. She majored in art history."

****

Lance knew for a fact he would NOT get along with Aurora Dawn's mother or her grandmother, and the farther away from them he stayed, the better for everyone. And if he saw her father and grandfather again, he might tear them apart for what they did to him—or had tried to do to him. *If* they recognized him. That wasn't likely. It was more than twenty years since they'd last seen him, and he looked even younger now.

"I hope you like hamburgers," Aurora Dawn said.

"I'm willing to give them a try."

Aurora Dawn laughed. "You mean you never ate a hamburger? Are you a vegetarian?"

"I don't know."

"You're funny. Well, I dare you not to love these hamburgers, and the nitrogen-infused milkshakes at this place are amazing. I especially love the Krispy Kreme shake."

"Krispy Kreme?"

"You have heard of Krispy Kreme doughnuts,

haven't you?"

"I haven't tasted one, no."

"I forgot. You're from Hungary."

"That's right."

"You may as well be from outer space. You've got a lot to learn."

Lance laughed. "I'm sure I couldn't have a better teacher."

Aurora Dawn turned up Lance's radio. A minute later, she turned it off and started singing. "Gosh darnit, Taylor. I heard half of your song and it's stuck in my head."

"Who's Taylor?" Lance wondered.

"Taylor Swift. You *have* heard of Taylor Swift, haven't you?"

Lance shrugged his shoulders.

"Let me put on some Johnny Cash. Surely you've heard of Johnny Cash."

Lance turned to her with a blank look on his face.

" 'Burning Ring of Fire'?" Aurora Dawn prompted, pulling a CD from her purse and inserting it into the car's CD player.

"Do you always carry music around with you?" he wondered.

"This is one of my favorites. I was listening to it in my room, and I was going to transfer it to my car."

Johnny's booming voice shook the car. "I fell into a burning ring of fire…"

They listened for a while.

"That's nice," said Lance. "I like that song."

Aurora Dawn smiled and pointed out the governor's mansion located right down the street from her house.

"Do you know the governor?" he asked.

"Of course. We're neighbors and family friends. We're driving along West Paces Ferry Road now. Our houses are in an area called Buckhead. It's one of the most prestigious areas in the city."

"Why do they call it Buckhead?"

"The man who used to own the land in the center of Buckhead ran a tavern, and there's a rumor that he killed a buck and hung its head on a post outside his establishment. So people started calling it "the buck's head.""

"I'm also a hunter."

"Really," said Aurora Dawn. "If you're hunting for things to do, Buckhead has some of the best shopping, dining, and entertainment in Atlanta or the Southeast."

"Good to know."

"Did you live in a big house in Hungary, too?"

"You ask a lot of questions."

"I'm a curious person. I want to know all about you. We don't have much time."

"Why?"

"Well, I uh, have an appointment with my mother. We have somewhere to be at three o'clock, so I need to be back home in time."

Lance glanced at his watch. "Well, then I'll talk fast. We lived in a castle in Hungary that had been in my family for decades. We moved here to downsize. Taxes, you know."

Aurora Dawn directed Lance to the restaurant, and as they drove, she pointed out the many streets with "Peachtree" in their names.

She glanced in his direction. "You know your new house is haunted, don't you?"

"I wasn't aware of that."

"Yes, your house was the scene of a horrific crime that happened when my mother was growing up. The house was invaded in the middle of the night and the family living there, including two young children, were murdered in their beds, while they slept. They never solved the case."

Lance wondered if his Maker was aware of the house's history or if he knew who the killers were. In fact, he wouldn't be surprised if his Maker was involved in the crime, since he had owned the house for decades.

Aurora Dawn interrupted his thoughts. "And I'm sure your mother is going to want to paint the outside. The color is hideous."

"I think she rather likes it the way it is," Lance said.

"Well, then your mother would get along with my grandmother. Fuchsia is her favorite color."

"I wouldn't dream of telling my mother what color to paint her house. She has her taste and I have mine, and I'm never going to meet Mark Twain."

Aurora Dawn wrinkled her nose and shot him a puzzled look. "What? Oh, you mean, 'never the twain shall meet.' I guess expressions are really different in Hungary."

"I don't want to talk about paint colors or my mother. Let's talk about you. You didn't always have blonde hair, did you?"

"How did you know? I was born with a head of coal black ringlets. But when I was two years old, it turned white blonde, and it's been blonde ever since."

Lance wanted to touch her hair, to pull it up to his

face and luxuriate in its smell of roses and vanilla, but instead, he pulled into the restaurant and parked the car. He went around to the passenger side and handed Aurora Dawn out of her seat.

"I'm impressed," she said.

"With what?"

"With how you treat a lady."

Lance locked the car, then put his hand on Aurora Dawn's back and guided her toward the restaurant.

"Let's sit outside," she said. "It's such a beautiful day."

"I would love that." Lance turned his head up to the sun and drank in the delicious warmth.

They were seated at a table, and the server handed them menus.

"Why don't you order for me since I'm unfamiliar with the menu," Lance suggested.

"Okay. Let's start with an order of the house potato chips. And then we'll each have the Double," she instructed the server and turned to Lance. "That's two Angus beef flip patties, with double bacon, double white American cheese, diced onions, pickles, and yellow mustard. How does that sound?"

"Wonderful." Lance's mouth watered.

The server brought water to the table, and they each ordered the Krispy Kreme shake.

Lance almost sighed when he tasted the potato chips.

"These are heavenly," he said.

"Wait till you taste the burgers. They're to die for."

"Not poisonous, I hope."

Aurora Dawn shook her head. "I forgot, you're from Hungary. You can't take everything I say literally.

It's just an expression. 'To die for' just means it tastes great. How old are you, anyway?"

Lance almost choked on a potato chip.

"Age is a relative thing."

"You didn't answer the question."

"Probably about the same age as you, twenty-four?" he guessed.

"That's exactly right. You just seem much older, more worldly."

"I've been around."

The server appeared with their lunch order.

Lance bit into his burger and said, "Oh, God."

"Is everything okay?" Aurora Dawn asked.

"I don't think I've tasted anything so delicious in my whole life. You're right. I *would* die for this."

Aurora Dawn laughed. "Now try the shake."

Lance sipped the shake through a straw and made a noise that sounded close to orgasmic.

"I would die for this, too," he said eagerly. "I never knew food could taste so good."

Before she knew it, the burger had disappeared from his plate.

"I think you inhaled that burger. You must have liked it."

"I want to do this again, soon. Can we come back tomorrow?"

"There are hundreds of places to eat. Let's try something new."

"So you'll go out with me again?"

Aurora Dawn met his eyes with a dangerous twinkle. "I'd like that."

"Since we don't have much time, let's go back to the car."

"I don't have to be back yet. So, okay."

"I don't want you to go. I'd like to be alone with you."

"Oh," she said, flustered.

He quickly paid the bill and took her hand, which generated an electric shock throughout his system.

They drove back to his house, and he pulled the car into the driveway. He turned off the motor. Reaching over the console, Lance anchored his hands on Aurora Dawn's face and kissed her. First softly, then more deeply, until their tongues tangled. He had planned to move at a slower pace, but there wasn't any time, and he needed to make her his.

Aurora Dawn's lips tasted like ambrosia—a concoction of honey and sugary Krispy Kreme shake. He moved his hands to her ears and massaged them. A few minutes of drugging kisses had her panting and trying to climb over the console to reach him. He pulled her onto his lap, kissed her some more, and her eyes widened when she felt his arousal.

He gambled and placed a hand under her T-shirt.

She didn't resist.

"Lance," she groaned.

"I want you, Aurora Dawn."

"Lance," she sighed, snuggling closer. "Your parents?"

"Not home. They're never home before dark."

They kissed some more and she wrapped her arms around him.

He pulled up her necklace. The amethyst glowed warm in his hand.

"What's this?"

"My grandmother gave it to me. It's for protection.

She warned me never to take it off."

"Protection against whom?"

"Anyone who would do me harm."

Lance scowled.

"What time is it?" she asked.

He looked at his watch. "It's two o'clock."

"I've got to go," she said pulling up her bra and pulling down her T-shirt.

"C-Can I call you?"

"I don't think that's a good idea." She grabbed her purse and rocketed out of the car.

"I moved too fast," he lamented.

"Not fast enough. It's not that. I wanted you just as much, but I haven't been completely honest."

She stood outside his car window. "My appointment. It's a dress fitting. A wedding dress. *My* wedding dress."

"I don't understand." He didn't want to understand.

"I'm getting married this weekend. To Bronx Bamberger. Goodbye, Lance."

Then she ran off down Lance's private driveway and wound up hers. She glanced back at him. He was still sitting in his car, staring after her. She threw him a kiss.

Then she ran into her house and almost straight into her mother.

"What happened to you? Your hair is all mussed up and your bra is on crooked. What did that boy do to you?"

"He cast some kind of spell on me. I wanted him so much, but I stopped it."

"What are you saying? That you cheated on Bronx?"

"Not really," Aurora Dawn said, grabbing her mother's hand and dancing her out to the garage. "We'd better leave now, or we'll be late for my fitting."

"We're not finished with this conversation, young lady."

Chapter Five

Lance paced the length of the ballroom in his new house. He wanted to fly, but flying was no longer in his wheelhouse. He'd climb the walls and walk on the ceiling if he could. But all he could do was scream out her name. *Aurora Dawn!* His heart pounded out of his chest like a hammer. He had trouble breathing. He was burning up. He wiped the perspiration off his clammy forehead. Was he ill? No, he was pretty sure it was worse than that. He was in love with the girl next door. He remembered the feeling. It was gnawing on his soul. He couldn't wait to see her again. It wasn't just a passing fancy. He *needed* to see her again. And soon.

He had to apologize for pushing her. Memories of her were imprinted on his brain. As far as Aurora Dawn knew, they had just met. But he had been waiting impatiently for this girl her whole life. And, like a wild boar, he'd practically attacked her. Would have feasted on her, if he were still Gedeon. But now he was powerless Lancelot Lakeland. Did he have any manners? Had he been raised by wolves? Pretty much. Werewolves and vampires.

Actually, he hadn't met his "parents" yet. His Maker had installed them as window dressing, to complete the perfect nuclear family. But *where* the hell were they? And *what* the hell were they? Vampires? Probably. One big happy vampire family in the witness protection program. Unbelievable.

He used his energy reserves to kick the couch. And in the process, banged the hell out of his toe. Now that he was mortal, he had to remember to be more careful with his body parts.

Aurora Dawn had held out hope, talked about another date, but then she told him about the wedding. *Her* wedding. He had five days to stop it, and stop it he would, if he had to kill her fiancé Bronx Bamberger. What kind of name was Bronx, anyway? No, he reminded himself. Civilized people, normal people, *good* people, did not kill. He needed to tamp down his baser instincts.

He would make her his or die trying. He couldn't afford to get this wrong. It was the only lifetime he had now. For the past few centuries he'd thought he would die of boredom. He didn't want to die of unrequited love.

Aurora Dawn! He screamed her name again, and the sound echoed off the walls.

The old Gedeon would have taken her right there in the car whether she was willing or not. He would have branded her as his own. But Lancelot Lakeland was a gentleman. Or was supposed to be. He had held his raw power in check when he kissed her but she was falling under his spell—or he under hers. Was it magic or was it real? He hoped it was real for her too.

Aurora Dawn was a talented sensitive who derived her power from the light. If she knew what he really was, knew *who* he really was, she would have nothing to do with him. And he wouldn't blame her. How could she forgive him if he couldn't even forgive himself?

His next move was key. An unexpected strike

while she was still susceptible and available. A whirlwind courtship. Gedeon would have dazzled her. Who knew what moves Lancelot Lakeland was capable of? Dejected, Lance walked into the living room and lay down on the couch. Closing his eyes, he summoned an image of Aurora Dawn. He imagined her offering a taut, pale breast, ripe for the taking. He was ravenous, and she was so real, he could almost taste her. He placed his hand on her nipple, and, using it for leverage, turned her, clasping her body against his to gain access to the real prize, her blue-veined, milky-white neck. He opened and closed his mouth against her salty sweet skin until he could feel her blood pulsing against his lips. And he, the reincarnated Gedeon, could do nothing but gum her like a teething baby, prompting a raw erotic memory.

Ignoring his urge to re-experience the joy, fascinating horror and yes, surprise, of his first kill, he cautioned himself to be gentle with his new love. He had to keep telling himself this wasn't Marika or Juliette.

"Settle down" would be his Maker's advice. "Don't rush." While the count had all the time in the world, he, Gedeon, aka Lancelot Lakeland, didn't. He wished the count had wiped his mind clean so he couldn't remember that he was inherently bad. So he could start over with Aurora Dawn. So his nerves and impulses weren't so raw. Was he even physically or mentally capable of goodness or tenderness? He would soon find out.

Chapter Six

Aurora Dawn glided out of the fitting room of the bridal shop and modeled the wedding dress for her mother.

Kate placed her hand over her heart as tears threatened to flow down her face. "It is absolutely beautiful. Aurora Dawn, you are a vision. Like Cinderella. Wait until Bronx sees you."

Aurora Dawn frowned. Bronx was not the man she was thinking about at this particular moment.

"That gown is lovely on you," agreed the saleslady.

"A Monique Lhullier would make anybody look lovely," Aurora Dawn replied modestly.

"You would look beautiful in any gown," Kate contradicted.

Aurora Dawn looked in the mirror. She was anything but vain, but gazing at her image in this a-line sweetheart blush Chantilly lace confection, she felt beautiful. If she didn't, then any number of glossy local magazines she picked up on the table in the shop would remind her. She was the most talked about, most written about bride-to-be of the season. "Angelic Aurora, Buckhead's Breathtaking Beauty to Wed," "Wedding Bells for Aphrodite in Atlanta," and "The World is Waking Up to a New Aurora Dawn" were just some of headlines used to describe her upcoming nuptials.

The saleslady fixed the veil with her mother's diamond tiara. She was wearing the shoes and jewelry bought to accessorize the dress, although the gown itself dazzled in its simplistic beauty.

Kate whipped out her iPhone and snapped some photos and made a video.

"Your father will love this. I can't believe my little angel is getting married."

"Mom," Aurora Dawn chided. "It's not like I'm leaving you. Bronx picked out a house for us on the same block. I'm sure I'll be seeing you every day."

"I know, but it's not the same."

What did she wish at this very moment? That Lancelot Lakeland could see her in her wedding gown. That she was going to walk down the aisle to meet Lancelot Lakeland and not Bronx Bamberger. She struck a sexy pose. "Mom, take another one and send it to my cell."

Kate snapped the pic.

Was that naughty? She would find out Lance's email and send it to him so he could see what he was missing—what they were missing.

"It looks perfect," announced the saleslady. "Your final fitting. Will you be taking the dress with you now?"

Kate nodded. "The wedding is this weekend."

Suddenly, Aurora Dawn felt tired and overwhelmed. Her heels were too high, her to-do list was too long, the diamond tiara dug into her scalp, and the wedding date was too close. "May I get undressed now?"

"Yes, let me help you," the saleslady said, following the bride-to-be into the dressing room while her mother went to pay the balance on the hefty bill. The dress was super expensive, but only a fraction of what the entire wedding was going to cost. Everyone had gone to so much trouble and expense on her account. Her mother was right. It was too late to cancel now. She would have no choice but to go through with it.

"Mom?" Aurora Dawn asked plaintively, slinking up to the cash register.

"Don't even think about it," Kate warned. "You're just getting some very natural pre-wedding jitters."

"But how do I know I'm doing the right thing?"

"You don't, not for sure. But Bronx is a good man. You've known him all your life. And I've known his father since we were kids."

Aurora Dawn sulked.

"You're not still thinking about that boy next door, are you?"

"Why do I even bother answering you? You always know what's in my head anyway. I'm exhausted."

"Let's get this dress home. You can put your feet up and rest."

"That sounds wonderful."

Chapter Seven

Aurora Dawn tore off the dress she had worn to the wedding shop and changed into tight jeans and a body-hugging T-shirt. She opened her bedroom window and let down her blonde tresses. She was loose and free, at least for the time being.

Lance was already at his window. He must have been watching for her. He stared over at her soulfully.

He couldn't hear her even if she shouted, so she pointed to the bottom of the driveway.

Lance was downstairs and out of his house in a flash, as if he wore wings.

Aurora Dawn ran down the driveway, came to a halt, and was transfixed by her neighbor's dreamy green eyes. He was as compelling as she remembered, with a killer body and the face of an angel. He absolutely overwhelmed her.

"Do you have a phone?" she asked.

"Right here. Why?" Lance removed a phone from the pocket of his jeans.

"Give me your number. I want to text you a picture."

Lance provided his number while Aurora Dawn tapped it in. He accessed his messages, and his jaw dropped when he saw what she'd sent.

"It's you, in your wedding dress. Y-you're so beautiful."

Suddenly, the wedding seemed real. Lance's face was sullen. "Why did you send this? To torture me?"

"To show you what you're missing."

Lance grumbled. "We need to go somewhere private."

"I don't think that's such a good idea," Aurora Dawn said.

Lance grabbed her hand and pulled her up the driveway. "Just to talk."

She entered the grand foyer of the Lakelands' Victorian mansion, glanced at the signature chandelier hanging from the vaulted ceiling, and sniffed the musty air. Various pieces of hideous furniture were scattered haphazardly throughout the dark room.

"Your mother is going to have her hands full redecorating. This place looks like something out of Dickens'—like Miss Havisham's mansion."

"I suppose that's an insult," Lance said, guiding her past the custom winding staircase and into the keeping room off the gourmet kitchen.

"I like the limestone fireplace, but let's just say the rest of the décor is not my style."

"It needs some work," Lance admitted.

"What it needs is some light," Aurora Dawn emphasized.

"And some mood music."

Lance went to the entertainment unit, and the room filled with the sound of swing.

"You like the '40s?"

"It was a good decade."

Aurora Dawn laughed. "How do you know? You weren't even born then."

Lance frowned. "I know what I like." He pulled

Aurora Dawn onto the couch beside him.

"Fair enough, Grandpa."

The front door opened and closed, followed by footsteps on the Carrara marble floors.

"I think we have company," said Aurora Dawn, pointing out the obvious.

Lance looked startled and rose from the couch.

A man and a woman resembling Morticia and Gomez from *The Addams Family* flew into the room.

"Lancelot!" the woman called, her voice strident. "Darling, we're finally here." She embraced him.

"Mother?" Lance coughed.

"Of course, darling, who else would I be?"

"Father, I presume," Lance whispered, shaking the stranger's hand.

Lance silently cursed the count. Why couldn't he have given him normal parents? Why did his family have to be so…theatrical?

"Mother, Father, I'd like you to meet Aurora Dawn Hale. She lives next door. Aurora Dawn, these people, who are obviously dressed for a costume party, are my parents."

Morticia kissed Aurora Dawn on both cheeks, and Gomez kissed her hand.

"How lovely to meet you, my dear," gushed Morticia. "Lancelot has told us so much about you."

Aurora Dawn caught Lance's attention, and he shrugged as she said, "We've only known each other a day."

"A day can be a lifetime when you're in love," Morticia expounded.

"Mother!" snarled Lance. *For Heaven's sake, woman, I've only just met you.*

"Oh, I've gone and spilled your little secret. Men can be so sensitive. Sorry, darling, but the way you waxed poetic about the girl, you made it sound like the sun rises and sets in her smile. I must say you didn't exaggerate. She's quite exquisite. Magnificent, really. No wonder you're so smitten."

"If I were only a few centuries younger—" Gomez sighed.

"Father!"

"Thank you, Mr. and Mrs. Lakeland," Aurora Dawn said, accepting the compliment graciously.

"Just call us Mom and Dad," Morticia said.

Aurora Dawn looked puzzled.

"Well, why wait? If you and my son are going to get married, there's no need to be so formal with each other."

"Mother, you don't understand," Lance corrected. "When I talked about a wedding, I meant that Aurora Dawn was getting married to *someone else*, this weekend, in fact."

Morticia was mortified. "But Lancelot, I thought that you—that she—I mean the way you talked about her—that you were a couple."

Lance flushed. "How could we be a couple when I just moved into the house and I've only just met Aurora Dawn *this morning*."

"When I met your mother, it was love at first sight," said Gomez. "I knew the minute I laid eyes on this ravenous beauty that I had to have her, and no one else, and I pursued her until she caught me."

"Darling, *mon coeur*," Morticia cooed, drawing her husband into a tender embrace.

"I thought you said you were Hungarian," Aurora

45

Dawn questioned.

"I was born in Hungary, but my parents are French." *I think.*

"Mom, Dad, do you think you can give Aurora Dawn and me some privacy? We have a lot to talk about."

"Of course you do, darling. You have a wedding to plan."

"*Aurora Dawn* has a wedding to plan," Lance corrected.

Morticia smiled slyly and took Aurora Dawn's elbow. "Don't be fooled, my dear. When my son wants something, he goes after it, and he always gets it. He's like his father in that regard. A one-track mind. And woe to the person or persons who get in his way. Your fiancé will be dispatched in a snap."

"Mother, please."

"No, darling, the girl might as well know what she's up against. My son has been mooning around like a lovesick cat all afternoon, waiting for you to come home."

"That's a lovesick cow," Aurora Dawn corrected.

"Cow, cat, what does it matter? Once a Lakeland mates, he mates for life, like a goose. And Lancelot has set his sights on you. We'll go now and leave you children alone to contemplate your future."

Lance blew out a breath of relief. "Thank you."

Morticia leaned into Lance and whispered. "How did we do?"

"Don't you think you're laying it on a little thick?"

"The count said we were to help you in any way we could."

"I think you've done enough for one day. We'll

talk later."

Morticia went to her husband's side. "Come along, darling. I think we have some *unpacking* to do in the bedroom."

Gomez's eyes lit up. "Yes, it's been a long trip. I'm very anxious to *unpack*."

After the couple left the room, Lancelot turned to Aurora Dawn.

"I apologize for my parents," Lance said. "Sometimes I feel like a third wheel with those two. They can't stop touching each other. It's embarrassing."

"My parents are the same way, they're so in love," said Aurora Dawn wistfully.

"Don't you feel the same way about your fiancé?"

Aurora Dawn tilted her head. "I've known Bronx all my life. I don't know how I feel about him. There aren't any sparks, if that's what you mean. If I were lying in bed in my negligee, and Bronx came into the bedroom naked, he'd be holding two cell phones and conducting business, and completely ignoring me."

"Has he done that?"

"Of course not. We haven't been together that way. I just know that business comes before pleasure for my fiancé."

Lance breathed a sigh of relief. "That would never happen with me." He gazed into Aurora Dawn's eyes, pulled her into his arms, and kissed her softly, then more intensely.

Aurora Dawn returned his passion. She felt dizzy. She thought she saw stars.

"You mean like the sparks I see and feel when I kiss you?" Lance posed, leading Aurora Dawn to the couch and pressing her lips against his until they were forehead to forehead and feverish with desire.

She nodded.

"Well, if we feel that way, don't you think we owe it to ourselves to see where this leads? Because once you're married, it's the end of the road for us."

Aurora Dawn raised her voice. "It shouldn't be the end of the road. It should be the glorious beginning."

"Not if you're trapped in a loveless marriage."

"How do you know if you're truly in love?"

"I think it must feel the way I feel whenever I look at you, the way I feel when you're not with me, the hungry need I have to possess you or I'll disintegrate."

"Show me, Lance. Show me how true love is supposed to feel."

Lance turned to Aurora Dawn and poured his love into her with a deepening kiss. She responded hungrily. He enfolded her in his arms, and she wound her arms around his neck. His lips traveled to her neck out of habit, and he nipped at her skin. She tasted sweet, but he no longer wanted to bite her. He wanted to possess her, body and soul. He wanted to be closer, as close as two people could be. He wanted her naked, bucking under him. His lips returned to hers, and he tasted her tongue. After several drugging kisses, he placed Aurora Dawn on her back and covered her with his body.

"Oh...my," Aurora Dawn said breathlessly, proof that his post-vampire manhood was still in working order. Some things never changed. He brushed up against her and freed himself. She reached down and took him in her hands. He could barely contain his excitement. In the past, he had been in total control of his body and his erection. But now he was a man, and if he wasn't inside of her soon, his "manhood" was going to spill out all over the hideous couch.

"Lance."

"Aurora Dawn." He unzipped her jeans and pulled them down around her feet. Then he pulled down her white lace panties. He lifted her T-shirt. She wasn't wearing a bra underneath, and he sucked on her nipple until he was wild with desire. He had slept with countless women through the centuries, sometimes more than one at the same time, but never did he want one as much as he desired Aurora Dawn at that moment.

He stuck his finger inside her to get her ready, but she was already wet and panting and thrashing restlessly.

"Lance," she moaned. He hoisted himself up and was about to enter her when her cell phone rang.

"Ignore it," he ordered as he prepared to plunge into her. The phone kept ringing.

"It's my mother."

"How the hell do you know that?" he said.

"I just do."

"Let it ring."

"She needs to talk to me."

"Aurora Dawn!"

"Lance," she said, her bottom lip quivering.

"What? Are you crying?"

"I've never—I want you but I've never done this before."

"Never done what?"

"This, what we're doing. I've never had sex before."

"Fuck." Lance pulled up, and his seed spilled out all over her. "Shit."

"Lance, I'm sorry."

"Christ, Aurora Dawn, I'm the one who's sorry. Why didn't you tell me?"

"It happened so fast, and I feel like I'm under a spell or something. I've never felt this way, not with Bronx, not with anyone. I've never acted this…wild, out of control."

He sat up and lifted her into his arms.

"My sweet Aurora Dawn. My angel of light. I'm so sorry. This is not the way I wanted it to be, our first time. But I couldn't help myself. I'm mad about you. I think it's you who has me under your spell. You're the sexiest, most bewitching woman I've ever known."

Tears spilled down Aurora Dawn's cheeks.

"It's okay," he soothed, kissing her tears away.

She hugged him tight. "I can't believe I let myself get so carried away. Look at me. I'm a sticky mess. I need to get cleaned up before your parents come back down."

"Don't worry about them. We don't want any of this to ruin such a magnificent couch."

Aurora Dawn laughed. Lance lifted her up and carried her to the guest bathroom and sat down on the side of the tub, still holding her.

"I will have you, you know. I have to. I'm in love with you."

Aurora Dawn bit her lip. "But you don't even *know* me."

"I know you, little one. I know all about you. I know you were meant for me and I was meant for you. I know I've been waiting my whole life for you. Now there's just the minor matter of what to do about Bronx."

Aurora Dawn look puzzled.

"Bronx. Your fiancé, remember?"

"I forgot about Bronx. What am I going to tell him?"

"We'll think of something. We'll tell him together. Do you love me?"

"I think I do," Aurora Dawn said and he kissed her, softly. "Let's get you cleaned up." Then he placed his hand on her breast. "God, what you do to me. Aurora Dawn, we have to talk."

The cell phone rang insistently.

"My mother is still trying to reach me."

"You'll call her back. Aurora Dawn, there are some things you don't know about me," Lance began, his lips tracing her forehead.

"I know how I feel about you."

"You're a pure person, Aurora Dawn. And I'm—"

"Right now, my thoughts are anything but pure, Lancelot Lakeland. And there are things you need to know about me, but I've got to go home now."

"I'll let you go for now, sweetheart, but promise me you'll come to me again tonight. Like Romeo and Juliet."

"Star-crossed lovers?"

"Eternally."

"I will. I promise."

Chapter Eight

"Kate, there's something I have to tell you." Jack paced the hardwood floors in their bedroom, his hands locked behind him.

"Aurora Dawn is not answering her phone, Jack." She stood transfixed staring out the bedroom window. Her face was lined with worry.

"I'm sure she's okay."

"No, she's not. She's with that boy next door. I'm afraid our daughter is in over her head."

Jack stopped in front of his wife, turned her to face him, and grasped her shoulders. "That's what I have to tell you. There *is* no one named Lancelot Lakeland. The man is a fraud. Or a ghost. His mother's name is Guinevere, Gwenn for short, and his father's name is Arthur, or Art, like Queen Guinevere and King Arthur in Camelot. That hardly sounds legitimate, and what kind of name is Lancelot Lakeland, anyway?"

"Is this someone's idea of a joke?" Her voice rose a pitch.

"A bad joke. I've been in Midtown at my old precinct, looking into our new neighbors. There's no record of them anywhere. There's no family by that name, no man by that name. They've appeared out of the blue without a trace, without a past, and now they're in the wind, and living next door to us."

"What do you mean, Jack?"

"I had to call in a lot of favors. I talked to my friend at the FBI, and he referred me to the U.S. Marshals Service, and it turns out our neighbors are off the grid."

She looked into his eyes. "I don't understand."

"They're in WITSEC, the witness protection program. I can't find out what case they've testified in or are going to testify in. It's very hush-hush, top secret, way above my pay grade, but it's obviously something serious, maybe a drug cartel or terrorist ring. And while I was there, I picked up the old case file for the death cult that murdered the family who used to live in their house. I doubt if there's a connection after so many years, but they've hired our firm to look into the cold case. It could be a coincidence, but I don't believe it."

"Jack, I feel like that boy is trying to separate Aurora Dawn from the herd. You know, like a defenseless fawn. We're her herd, Jack. We need to circle around her. Do you think our daughter could be in danger?"

"Our daughter is anything but defenseless, Kate. But why take a chance? She's smart and she's savvy. But maybe a little reckless. Let's invite them all over for dinner and take a look for ourselves. See what all the fuss is about."

"Honey, the wedding is in four days. I don't have time to plan a dinner party."

"It doesn't have to be a party, Kate, just a simple dinner. Then you and your mother can do your voodoo magic and form your own opinions."

"Jack, you're hopeless." She ran her hands down his arms, kissed him and sighed. "All right, I'll arrange it."

Aurora Dawn swept into the room.

"What have you been up to?" Kate asked.

"No good," Aurora Dawn answered sweetly.

"Well, I just wanted you to know that we're going to invite the Lakelands to dinner tonight, Lancelot and his mother and father."

"Do you really have time for that?"

"Not really, but it seems to me that if you have genuine feelings for that boy, and it's obvious that you do, we want to meet him."

"To size him up?"

"Why not?" Jack said. "We're going to put the whole lot of them under a microscope."

"Daddy!" Aurora Dawn protested.

"Your father's right. We're just trying to protect you, and we don't want anything to sabotage this wedding. So tell me, what are his parents like?"

Aurora Dawn shook her head. "They look a lot like Morticia and Gomez in *The Addams Family*."

Kate laughed nervously. "What about the house?"

"The place is dark, medieval almost. The only thing it's missing is a moat and a drawbridge."

"Surely, they're going to repaint," Jack said.

"No, he says his mother likes the color."

****

"Lance, we've just been invited to dinner at the Hales' house next door," said Gwenn.

"We can't go over there. I can't face Aurora Dawn's mother and grandmother. What if they recognize me?"

"We'll cross that drawbridge when we come to it. Do you love the girl? More to the point, do you want her?"

"Of course."

"If you're serious about her, you're going to have to meet her parents eventually. You'll win them over." Gwenn grabbed Lance's chin between her fingers and tilted his face. "By the way, that's a beautiful tan you've got there, son. Sure beats my sprayed-on version to hell."

Lance glanced into the hallway mirror, tipped his head back remembering the warm heat on his face, and smiled. "We ate lunch in the sun and drove in the car with the top down."

"What's that like?"

"Glorious. Like nothing I've ever experienced before. It felt like freedom."

"I forgot to ask. How did things go this afternoon? I heard a lot of grunting and groaning down there. Did you seal the deal?"

Lance paled. "Not exactly. It was a little premature. *I* was a little premature."

"That doesn't sound like you. As I hear it, you were quite the ladies' man. *Hard* to resist, with stamina to spare. You have quite a reputation with the ladies."

Lance shrugged. "I found out, at the last minute, my lady is a virgin."

Gwenn blew on her nails to dry them. "I didn't know there were any of those still around. And since when has that ever stopped you? In fact, I thought you liked them fresh and frightened, hot and helpless."

"Things are different with Aurora Dawn. I wasn't about to force her."

"You could have glamoured her."

"I would never do that!"

"Now, that really doesn't sound like you. You used

to razzle-dazzle with the best of them."

"Chicago is her favorite musical," Arthur explained.

Lance grimaced. Where did the count get these two from—central casting?

"I've changed," Lance explained. "Even if I wanted to, I don't have those powers anymore."

"But *we* do. And the count said we were to do *anything* we could to help you in your quest."

"I'd be glad to hold the wildcat down," Arthur offered graciously.

Gwenn glared at her husband.

"Father! I don't want that kind of help. I want to win her on my own. What time are we expected for dinner?"

"Seven," his mother answered.

Lance turned to Gwenn. "There is one thing you can do."

"Anything, darling."

"Wear something a little less *dramatic*."

"Of course. We won't embarrass you. We'll be plain waspy Gwenn and Art Lakeland from France. We'll help you get your happy ending."

Chapter Nine

The door chime sounded, and Kate went to the entrance. She didn't know what she was expecting, certainly not the two normal people standing before her as she opened the door.

Guinevere reached out and shook Kate's hand. "It was so nice of you to have us. I'm Gwenn, and this is my husband, Art."

Kate stood in the foyer speechless until Jack came up behind her and touched her shoulder. She regained her composure. "Gwenn and Art, so nice to meet our new neighbors. And this is my husband, Jackson Hale—Jack."

Aurora Dawn stood beside her father.

"And I understand you've already met our daughter, Aurora Dawn."

"That's right," answered Gwenn. "We had the pleasure of meeting her this afternoon. She's lovely."

Kate beamed. "She's going to make a beautiful bride."

Aurora Dawn peeked around the door. "Where's Lance?"

"He's right behind us. He wanted to make a good impression, so he's going through his wardrobe like a nervous schoolboy."

"Mother." Lance's lowered his single brow in reproof.

"Lance, you look wonderful," Aurora Dawn gushed. "I'd like you to meet my parents, Katherine and Jack Hale. "Mom, Dad, this is Lance."

Lance stood there, his hands in his pockets, locked in position, gazing at Aurora Dawn, who pulled him inside, almost knocking him over.

Aurora Dawn was dressed in a pale yellow silk dress, with matching yellow heels. Her hair flowed loosely around her shoulders.

"You look—so beautiful, like a vision, like a princess," Lance said, transfixed.

"Thank you. My grandparents are waiting in the dining room."

"Why don't we all head that way," Jack suggested. "What can I get you folks to drink?"

"Just water for us," Art answered.

"It's already on the table," Kate said.

Kate introduced the new neighbors to Juliette and Will.

"Aurora Dawn tells us you're from France," Juliette began. "What interesting names—Guinevere, Arthur, and Lancelot."

"We could say the same of you—Juliette." Gwenn's voice dripped with sarcasm. "There must be a Romeo around here somewhere."

Juliette scowled.

Everyone took their seats around the table. Aurora Dawn sat next to Lance, and their hands found each other under the table.

"I didn't have much time to prepare. I pretty much threw this meal together," Kate apologized.

"Don't let my wife fool you. She's a wonderful cook."

"I've made a roast chicken with onions and garlic," Kate said as she brought the platter to the table. "And I've roasted some asparagus with sea salt and black pepper, and we also have baked potatoes. I hope you like it."

No one made a move to take any food.

Lance caught his mother's attention and raised his eyebrow.

"It all looks so delicious, Kate," Gwenn said. "But we're not really hungry. Art and I are on a liquid diet."

Lance reached out and filled his plate. "I'm starving. That will leave more food for me."

Jack followed, then Kate, Juliette and Will, and Aurora Dawn.

"Would you like a soda or anything else to drink?" Kate asked.

"No, thank you," answered Art. "We're just so glad you invited us."

Kate, Jack, Lance, and Aurora Dawn ate in silence. Juliette picked at her food while she sized up the new neighbors. Will stared helplessly at Juliette.

"Mrs. Hale, this chicken is delicious. I may have seconds."

"There's plenty, so feel free. And save room for dessert. I made some key lime pie."

"I wish you hadn't gone to so much trouble," Gwenn said.

"It was no trouble."

"So what do you do for a living?" Juliette asked Art.

"Oh, we don't work," answered Gwenn. "We're retired. We just travel."

"Why did you move to Atlanta?" Juliette continued

the grilling.

Gwenn took a drink of water. "Because it has such a fantastic airport."

"A great reason, Mrs. Lakeland," agreed Jack.

"Don't they say you can't get to heaven without going through Atlanta?" Art added.

"That's what they say," agreed Kate, in an effort to keep the conversation going.

Juliette excused herself. When she returned, she placed a birthday cake with purple frosting on the table. "In all the excitement of the wedding, my daughter forgot it was her birthday."

"How old are you, Kate?" Gwenn asked.

"I'm afraid it's fifty-four."

"I don't know anybody that old," Juliette said. "You must be mistaken."

"You look as beautiful as the day I met you, honey," said Jack, getting up from the table to kiss Kate. Juliette lit the candles and everyone began to sing 'Happy Birthday.' "

"Now make a wish," Juliette prodded.

Kate closed her eyes for a moment and then blew out the candles.

Aurora Dawn didn't have to imagine what her mother wished for. She wished the wedding would go off without a hitch. She loved her mother, but she didn't know if she could make her wish come true.

At the end of the meal, Aurora Dawn announced she was going to walk Lance home.

"Don't stay out too late," Kate cautioned. "We have a million errands to run tomorrow."

Aurora Dawn glanced at her mother and then grabbed Lance's hand and led him out the door. His parents followed.

****

The Hales and the Bradleys gathered in the living room.

Jack was the first to speak. "Well, that was strange."

"I'll say," said Kate. "They were on a liquid diet? What was that all about? If they weren't going to eat, why did they agree to come over for dinner?"

"For the kids, I guess," Jack reasoned. "Well, what's the verdict?"

"Did you notice how they avoided my questions about their time in Hungary? Those people are no more French than I am," Kate said. "They were very vague. Mom, did you get a reading on Lance?"

Juliette paused. "He's an old soul. He's totally blocking me. I don't get the sense that he's evil so much as he's conflicted. Good and evil are warring within him. I can see why Aurora Dawn is attracted to him. You can't deny he's seriously sexy."

"I'll drink to that," Kate agreed, taking a sip of her cocktail. "When Lancelot and I were discussing artwork, he was specific about some pieces that we know were stolen during the war and since returned to their rightful owners." She looked pointedly at Juliette.

"I noticed that as well. He's quite conversant about art."

"But no one but a select few would be aware that those pieces we referred to were stolen."

"Correct. And the boy is from Hungary. Wasn't Gedeon Nagy from Hungary?"

The room fell silent.

"That would be quite a coincidence, Jack, and we

all know you don't believe in…them," Will commented.

Jack flexed his fist and looked at his business partner. "Lance can't be the same man we killed. That was more than twenty years ago, and that man was at least forty years old. Lance is not much more than twenty himself—I think Aurora Dawn mentioned they were the same age. How is that possible?"

"And Gedeon Nagy was a beast," Kate pointed out. "How can he be the same man who looks at our daughter like she's the sun and the moon and the stars? It's obvious he's smitten with her. It's just poor timing."

"I'm convinced his feelings for her are genuine. There's no doubt. And yet—"

"Mother, he can't be a vampire. There are no such things."

Juliette sighed. "I've seen a lot in my life that cannot be denied."

"They all looked normal to me," Will observed.

"They looked normal and they dressed normal, but 'Queen Guinevere' and 'King Arthur' were giving off a weird vibe," Juliette pointed out.

Kate cleared her throat and knocked back the rest of her drink. "And we're ignoring the elephant in the room. No matter who he is and who they are, our daughter is getting married this weekend to one man, and she's head over heels in love with another man. That's what we need to focus on."

"I'm going to have a heart-to-heart talk with that boy," Jack insisted.

Kate raised her empty glass and addressed the group. "And what about poor Bronx? He has no idea someone is trying to steal his fiancé right out from under him on the eve of their wedding. He won't take that lightly."

"One thing we can all agree on is that Bronx is anything but poor," Juliette said, and they all laughed.

"This is not a joke," Kate said, trying not to smile. "This wedding is going to happen. The question is, who will be the groom?"

"Surely Aurora Dawn has enough sense to know she can't continue this behavior," Juliette said. "She's out of control. She's in love. I recognize the signs."

"I think it's more that she's in lust. And what does true love have to do with good sense?" Kate punctuated her statement by banging her crystal wine glass on the coffee table before she stood up and wobbled.

Jack caught his wife by the elbow to keep her from slipping. "Kate, I think we'd better get the birthday girl to bed." Jack's eyes gazed into Katherine's as he rubbed her arm sensuously, his desire evident. "It's been a long day. Will, you and I need to talk in the morning. These people aren't who they say they are. We've got to get to the bottom of this, and soon."

Jack wound his arm around Kate and led her up the stairs to their bedroom.

"Kate's going to get lucky tonight," Juliette whispered, recognizing the signs.

Will placed a soft kiss on his wife's lips. "So is her mother."

Chapter Ten

"How's the other half of Atlanta's newest power couple?" Bronx asked as he sat on the flowered couch in the formal living room of the Crystal Palace.

"Are you here to check on your investment?"

"Don't be ridiculous," said Bronx as he fingered Aurora Dawn's curls. "You're wearing your hair up tomorrow night, aren't you? It makes you look more sophisticated. That's what I told the woman from *Town & Country*."

"I can't believe you're so concerned about my hair. And you've got to stop talking about us as a power couple. It's unseemly."

"Baby, you can't deny it. You're just nervous about the wedding night. I understand that. But I promise you have nothing to worry about. I've got it all under control. You're going to be fine. I'll be with you every step of the way."

Aurora Dawn rolled her eyes. "Bronx, do you love me, really love *me*, not the idea of me or my fortune or the Crystal name? You can be honest. We've known each other all our lives."

"Baby, how can you ask that?"

"Because I need to know. Am I the greatest love of your life? Am I your soulmate?"

"That's crazy talk. We're getting married. That's all you need to know."

"Yes, but would you leap to death in woe for me? Would you ever rescue me in the wood?"

"Have you been watching *Camelot* on Netflix again?"

Aurora Dawn pursed her lips.

"Life is not a fairy tale, Aurora Dawn. I'm not a knight in shining armor, and you're not a princess in a castle, although your parents have raised you like one. Your head is always in the clouds. It's all those vampire stories you write. They're giving you unrealistic ideas and expectations. That's all going to stop after we're married."

"I thought you liked my stories."

"Well, yes, but I don't want you turning out like your grandmother."

"Or my mother. Go ahead and say it. Like my mother."

"Crystal Ball Kate? I rest my case. She's a psychic. I don't want to be married to a psychic. And I don't want a bunch of psychic children running around the house tunneling into my thoughts."

Aurora Dawn blew out a breath. "I know that. I can read your mind, Bronx."

"That's because we've grown up together. We can finish each other's sentences. But you're not a psychic. My father says that your mother—"

"Let me finish your sentence. Your mother was the love of his life, but her psychic abilities scared the hell of him, and that's why he broke it off. The truth is, my mother was not in love with your father. My mother fell head over heels in love with my father. And that's the way I want to feel about the man I marry. I don't think that's unreasonable, Bronx Bamberger.

"And while we're on the subject of mothers. Your mother is the original Momzilla-in-Law. I've gone along with almost everything she's wanted. We're having two officiants, a rabbi *and* a reverend. I drew the line when she wanted to release white doves after the ceremony, *inside* our house. And wasn't it Betsey Bamberger who said, "Do you think it's over the top to have a chandelier under the chuppah?"

"I thought you wanted a traditional wedding."

"Yes, I wanted fairy lights under the chuppah, not a chandelier."

"And we won that round, didn't we, darling?"

"I'm keeping score, Bronx. It's Betsey Bamberger 19, Aurora Dawn Hale 3. This wedding is getting out of hand. Your mother thinks it's her wedding, but she's the mother of the groom."

"Betsey Bamberger cannot be denied. And you know your mother is just as invested in *our* wedding."

"We should have just eloped or had a destination wedding, but I have a feeling Betsey would have come along on our honeymoon."

"Now, I don't think you're being fair. Betsey got us into *Town & Country.*"

"I don't care about *Town & Country.*"

"That's bordering on sacrilegious."

Aurora Dawn grabbed Bronx's hands. "Kiss me."

"Now?"

"Yes, now."

Bronx shrugged and kissed Aurora Dawn's lips lightly.

"No, kiss me like you mean it."

Bronx put his arms around her and kissed her, and she felt...nothing. It was like kissing her brother. Her pulse didn't race. Her heart didn't yearn. Her toes didn't curl like they did when Lance kissed her, leaving her feeling feverish, wanton, wanting more.

She removed Bronx's arms from around her waist. "What did you feel when you kissed me?"

"Feel? It was a kiss. What are you getting at? If you're looking for *true love* like they feed you in those romance novels you read and the chick flicks you watch, you know that's a bunch of nonsense. People don't feel that way in real life."

Aurora Dawn folded her arms across her waist and tapped her foot. "Why do you want to marry me, Bronx?"

"Like you said, we've known each other all our lives. Our parents are best friends. They expected it. This was always the plan."

His words weren't making her feel any better.

"How do you think it will be between us, when we finally, you know, make love?"

"You mean will the earth move?"

"Something like that."

"It will be sex. Sex is always great."

"In your vast experience?"

"I never lied to you. You know I've been with other women."

"Yes, so you keep reminding me. But what was it like with them?"

"I don't think we should be talking about sex with other women the day before our wedding."

"I think we need to."

"What is it you want to hear? That it was off-the-charts great? That it was fucking amazing? For a guy, it always is."

"Do you think it will be *fucking* amazing for us?" Aurora Dawn whispered softly, near tears.

"That's different. You're going to be my wife. Sex between us won't be dirty."

"Dirty? Why should it be any different? Why shouldn't you enjoy having sex with me? Why shouldn't I enjoy it?"

"Because you'll be my wife! Where are you going with this, Aurora Dawn?"

"I have the feeling you regard our wedding as a merger—the Crystal fortune and the Bamberger fortune, together at last. That we'll be the perfect couple on the social scene, but what about in the bedroom? Will we be compatible in the bedroom, Bronx?"

"We could try it out before the wedding."

"That won't be happening."

"Do you want me to be honest?"

"That would be nice."

"Aurora Dawn, sure, I like the idea of us. We're going to rule the world."

"What if I don't want to rule the world?" Aurora Dawn asked quietly.

"Then you'll stand by my side while I do. Baby, we're perfectly suited for each other in every way."

Aurora Dawn mumbled, "Are we?"

"What did you say?"

"Nothing. I—is there anything you want me to pick up for you before the wedding, anything I can do?"

"No, I think I've got it covered. I just picked up my tux on the way over here. So the next time I see you will be at the rehearsal dinner, the day before you become Mrs. Bronx Bamberger. We're doing coordinating outfits, right? You're wearing the Tadashi Shoji mint cotton and nylon embroidered-lace dress, and my suit will have a tie in a complementary color. The same color theme as the table arrangements."

"Bronx, you're too concerned about how we look—how I look—and whether or not we coordinate. What does that matter?"

"It matters, future Mrs. Bamberger, because *Town & Country* magazine is doing a feature spread on our wedding. I told you that. Or I told your mother. The fashion editor was particularly interested in what you were going to wear Friday night. She could care less about me. You're the main attraction."

"That's the silliest thing I ever heard. Next, you're going to want to see me in my wedding dress before the ceremony."

"I wouldn't dream of breaking with tradition," Bronx said. "I know how important it is to you to have a fairy tale wedding."

Bronx placed a quick kiss on Aurora Dawn's lips on his way out the door before she could come up with a sufficiently sassy response.

Aurora Dawn cast her eyes to the floor and summoned up the image of Lance's mouth and the feeling of his last searing kiss on her lips. Her lips had been on fire then. Her stomach had plummeted like a falling elevator. In comparison, Bronx's peck on her lips left her cold and disappointed and stuck in first gear.

Sex wasn't that important, was it? How would she know? She'd never lost control of her feelings before. Before Lance Lakeland appeared in the picture.

Chapter Eleven

"Kate, I got a call about—"

"Jack, don't tell me. You promised you wouldn't take another case before the wedding. You've been working so hard lately. I need your full attention to get through this weekend. You have no idea how much work goes into planning a—"

"I haven't even told you what it's about."

"I know what it's about. It's another serial killer, another kidnapping, another disaster that only you can solve. Am I right? That's what our lives have been about for nearly twenty-five years."

Jack placed his hand on his wife's shoulder. "Kate, it's a thirteen-year-old boy. He's gone missing. From right down the street. The police need our help. I need your help."

Kate sighed and resigned herself to hearing about a new case. "Tell me."

"It's the little Bader boy on the next block. Someone came in through his bedroom window in the middle of the night and took him from his room. But there is no sign of forcible entry. No rope, no evidence a ladder was used. No DNA. It's as if someone flew in the window and snatched him from his bed. His parents are frantic. You know how close the governor is with the Baders. He's demanding immediate action. He wants us to get the boy back sooner rather than later.

The election is coming up."

"That's horrible. But isn't that the job of the police department?"

"Of course the police have been called in, but the governor insists that we're on the team. He wants us involved. More to the point, he wants *you* involved. And what the governor wants, the mayor wants. We have an advantage because we know the Baders. They'll talk to us. Aurora Dawn used to babysit Trent Bader. The mayor knows we can solve this case and bring the boy home. He knows we'll be discreet. He doesn't want this to turn into a media circus."

"You mean like every other case we're involved in?"

"Yes. He doesn't want to alarm the community. He just wants to bring the boy home safe to his family. Hopefully, this is an isolated incident, not a pattern."

Kate expelled a breath and tried not to run through the growing list of things that had to be accomplished before the wedding—make sure the gifts for the out-of-town hotel guests were delivered, give the caterer the final head count for the dinner, approve the budget for the breakfast at the Atlanta Botanical Garden, check on the place cards for the reception, to name a few. Oh, and confirm the flowers, the band, and the videographer. The contracts were all finalized more than a year ago. She and Bronx's mother had been planning this wedding practically since the kids were infants. She had a wedding planner, but insisted on being consulted about every detail. Had all the bridesmaids picked up their gowns? She had to remember to ask Aurora Dawn.

"Kate, have I lost you?"

"Sorry, I just have so much on my mind with the wedding. We probably should have had it at a hotel." She changed gears. "What do we have to work with? Clothes from the victim? Any clues at all?"

Jack handed a paper bag to Kate.

"There's a shirt of his that he last wore. He was snatched in his pajamas. Kate, a thirteen-year-old boy. Who would do that?"

"A degenerate sadist. A criminal. The kind of person you bring into our home on a daily basis."

"I've never brought a criminal into our home," Jack objected fervently.

"But you bring the files home, and then I can't get the horrible images out of my mind. The death scenes, the blood, the murder weapons, the running trail of innocents."

Jack folded Kate in his arms and placed a kiss on the top of her head. "Kate, I'm sorry. I didn't realize you felt that way. I know you're particularly sensitive to evil, and I know how these cases affect you. We've been working together for twenty-four years. I couldn't do my job without you. I'd be nothing without you. You know that."

Kate placed her arms around Jack's waist and hugged him close. "And I couldn't live without you. I'll let Mother and Will know where we'll be. Should we ask them for their help?"

"Will is about to retire from the business. I hate to bother him."

"I know. But he'll feel left out if we don't involve him."

"We need to go see the Baders. They've agreed to talk to us. After we get more information, we can bring in Will and Juliette."

"Has there been a ransom note? Or any contact from the kidnappers?"

"Nothing yet. Their phones are tapped. The police are with them now. It's probably about the money. The Baders are one of the wealthiest families in Atlanta."

"It's not always about money," Kate pointed out. "When are we expected?"

"As soon as possible."

"Well, then we'd better go." Kate followed Jack to the garage and into their black Lexus SUV.

Jack backed the car out, then sent it across the circular driveway and toward the entrance gate. It took only minutes down a side street to reach their destination.

As they approached the Bader estate, a police officer stationed at the bottom of the driveway recognized Jack and waved them in. Another officer stood at the entrance to the house, and he let them pass.

When they entered the house, the Baders were seated on the couch, staring at the phone. Felicia Bader's face was puffy and furrowed with mascara tracks.

Kate came around to her and hugged her friend. Jack shook hands with Barnaby Bader.

"I'm so sorry, Felicia," Kate began. "Have you slept at all?"

"I can't sleep. I can't eat. I just want him to come home."

"Of course. Felicia, can we see Trent's room?"

"I need to stick by the phone in case someone calls," explained Barnaby.

"We'll be right back," Jack assured him.

Felicia led Kate and Jack up the stairs to her son's bedroom on the second floor.

They approached the room reverently. This was the last place the boy had been seen. The Harry Potter comforter was on the floor. Clothes were scattered on a chair near the window. Kate walked around the bedroom and into the closet, touching everything. She stood quietly in the center of the room.

"Was anything taken?" Kate asked.

Felicia's eyes welled up, a sure sign the waterworks were about to flow.

"I mean besides Trent."

Felicia wiped her eyes. "His favorite toy, a stuffed rabbit. He's had it since he was a baby. He wouldn't go anywhere without Mr. Bunny. Of course, he didn't know that we knew he slept with it every night, still does, but it's gone. He must have grabbed it when he was abducted."

Jack touched Felicia's shoulder. "Are you sure he was abducted? Could he possibly have run away to meet a friend?"

"Jack, you know Trent. He's not the kind of kid who would do that. He's a good boy."

"Running away doesn't make him bad. It's something a teenager might do, especially a boy. I did it myself when I was Trent's age."

"Have you talked to any of his friends?" Kate asked.

"Yes, Barnaby has called them all, talked to the boys and their parents, and there's nothing. No clue about what could have happened to him. None of this makes any sense, Kate. I mean if they want money, why haven't they called? Why didn't they leave a note?

74

Why did they take my little boy?"

"Has he had any trouble at school?" Kate wondered. "Was anything bothering him?"

Felicia sighed. "He did mention some bullying, some kids at school sending messages on his computer. Do you think that had anything to do with his disappearance?"

"We have to cover all the bases," Kate said. "Jack will have someone go through his computer."

Jack shifted back and forth and faced Felicia. "Did you have an argument earlier this evening?"

"Of course not."

"Can you remember the last thing he said to you?" Kate prodded gently.

Felicia laughed before the tears started flowing again.

"When I tucked him in he said, 'Mom, I'm a thrill seeker, so you don't need to try to control me.' I replied, 'Is that right? Let me know how that works out for you!' He is so precocious. He says the funniest things. We laughed about it. Then I kissed him on the forehead like I always do and turned out the light, and that's the last time I saw my precious little boy. Jack, Kate, you have to find him before—you just have to find him. He's so young and vulnerable."

"We are going to do everything we can," Jack assured Felicia.

Felicia wrung her hands and rubbed them across her face. "Kate, I'm so sorry. I forgot to ask. How are the wedding plans coming? I don't think we'll be able to attend unless—"

"Don't worry about the wedding. Just focus on Trent."

Kate kissed Felicia and left the house with Jack.

When they got outside, Jack asked. "Well, what do you think?"

"He's alive, Jack. I can feel it. And he's close. But he's in danger. We have to get to him. He's running out of time. Drive me around the neighborhood. First stop, the cemetery. All the boys in the neighborhood used to play there."

Jack helped Kate into the car and headed down the driveway and onto West Paces Ferry Road, the wide street dotted with mansions, probably the wealthiest thoroughfare in Atlanta. He pulled into the cemetery.

Truthfully, the place scared the bejeezus out of him. But he had to admit it would have an attraction to a thirteen-year-old runaway. Jack steered the car slowly around the property. There was a full moon, which made the place even more eerie. No sign of the boy here.

Kate closed her eyes and focused on the missing little boy as Jack exited the cemetery and drove slowly around their block. When they passed the house next door to the Crystal Palace, Kate's eyes flew open. "Stop the car. He was here."

"Here? You mean right next door to us? Where the Lakelands live?"

"Yes," Kate insisted.

"He's here now?"

Kate hesitated. "He was. I don't know. He is or he was. I'm getting a strong signal."

"Let me drive up the driveway." Jack dimmed the lights as the car crawled up the steep incline.

"What are our new neighbors going to think?"

"If they ask, we drove up the wrong driveway by

mistake."

"Pretty unlikely," Kate said. "I've lived here my whole life. I wouldn't make that mistake."

Kate pressed Trent's shirt against her face and breathed in his little boy scent. "But the child needs our help. He's here or around here."

"You're right. We can't just knock on the door," Jack said. "It's too late at night."

"What do you suggest?"

"I'll turn around. Let's go home and see if Aurora Dawn can pay a late night visit to the Lakelands, to Lance in particular."

"The less she sees of that boy, the better," Kate objected. "She's confused enough already, and I hate to get Aurora Dawn mixed up in a murder investigation."

"It's not murder, yet," Jack reasoned. "Aurora Dawn has better instincts than I do. Let her sniff around."

Kate bristled. "You really want to throw those two together? The wedding is only days away. That boy is going to suck the light out of our daughter."

"I don't think we have a choice, Kate. A little boy's life is in danger, and Aurora Dawn needs to make up her mind. I don't want her to live a lifetime of regret."

"Neither do I, but her life was so well ordered. Everything was working out. I thought—"

"Look, Kate. I like Bronx well enough, but he reminds me of his father. And you know what I think of that man."

"You're not still jealous?"

"That you almost married him? And that he still has the hots for you?"

"Jack, I'm a middle-aged woman. No one has the hots for me."

Jack reached over and squeezed Kate's closest breast. "I do."

"Jack!"

"I can't fondle my own wife in my own car?"

"This is not the time or the place. Let's just get home."

Within minutes, Jack and Kate were sitting on the living room couch, watching Aurora Dawn descend the stairs.

"Just think, in three days, I'll be walking my little girl down those stairs in her wedding dress," Jack whispered to Kate.

"God willing."

"What are you two whispering about," Aurora Dawn asked.

"Honey, we need your help."

"What is it, Dad?"

"You remember the Bader boy. You used to babysit him."

"Of course. Has something happened to Trent?"

"Well, he's gone missing, and your mother and I have been asked to help find him."

"Missing? What do you mean?"

"Well, someone took him from his bedroom or he ran away. And your mother thinks—I mean, she feels strongly—she's getting a signal that he may be or may have been in the house next door."

"At the Lakelands'?"

"Yes," Kate answered.

"But that makes no sense. What would he be doing there?"

"We don't know, but we thought—that is, I thought—you might call Lance and go over there and have a look around, see what you can see."

"You want me to spy on Lance and his family?"

"Not spy, exactly."

"I'm against it, Aurora Dawn. I don't think you should be around that boy this close to your wedding. That's tempting fate."

"You really think it would do any good to go over there? I can hardly come right out and ask him if he's stashed a missing boy at his house."

"Ask him to give you a tour of the house," Jack suggested.

Aurora Dawn looked at her cell phone. "At eleven o'clock at night? Mom, do you really think he's over there?"

"Perhaps he just wandered off to explore, like boys do, to have a look at the new neighbors?" Kate said halfheartedly.

"Through a locked window with the alarm set?" Jack interrupted. "He hardly wandered off, Kate. He was abducted."

"Mom?"

Kate flexed her hand. "Your father is right. The child was stolen from his bed, taken against his will. I don't know for sure he's there, but my strong feeling is that he was. I think he's passed out. He's not dead, but he's in trouble. I can feel it in here." Kate pressed a palm against her heart.

Aurora Dawn walked toward the door. "Then I'll go. Let me just call Lance so he knows I'm coming. I'm not going to lie to him."

Aurora Dawn pressed a button on her phone.

"Lance, I'd like to come over now, if it's all right with you. We need to talk. A little boy in the neighborhood has gone missing, and I'm frightened. I don't want to be alone."

Aurora Dawn spoke for another minute and then broke the connection.

"What did he say?" Kate asked.

"He can't wait to see me. He wondered if you and Daddy were at home. He sounded genuinely worried about me."

Kate looked at Jack and frowned. "Be careful, honey."

Chapter Twelve

"Mother, is that blood on your lips?"

Gwenn sucked the tiny red droplet onto her tongue. "I'm just recovering from gum surgery."

Lance frowned. "Have you been hunting again?"

"A girl's gotta eat."

"I hope you're not trolling in the neighborhood."

"I won't do it again, I promise."

"There's a little boy gone missing down the block. You don't have anything to do with his disappearance, do you? We're not going to find his body drained and dumped in a vacant field somewhere, are we?"

Gwenn glared at Lance. "I'm not a savage, Lance. I don't hunt children."

Lance exhaled and held out a yellow well-worn stuffed bunny that had seen better days.

"Then what was *this* doing on the basement stairs?"

"How should I know? It probably belonged to the previous owners."

Lance stroked the rabbit. "Did you know the previous owners?"

"Of course not."

"Did the count?"

Gwenn stared at the ceiling. "You'll have to ask him. Since when have you become so respectable? I've heard stories about you, back in the nineteen-forties, remember?"

"Those were dark days. I'm turning my life around. I'm not that person anymore."

"Well, you could be a bit more understanding."

"I do understand. But you have to understand this is my last chance for happiness. I don't want to think about those days, about the horrific things I did. I don't have those tendencies anymore. You do what you have to do, but don't flaunt it, for goodness' sake."

"What does goodness have to do with it?"

"It has everything to do with it. I want to be a worthy mate for Aurora Dawn. I want to come to her fresh and clean on our wedding day."

"I'm all about making Count Nagy happy, but you seem to forget one important detail. The girl is engaged to someone else. What are you going to do about him? The old Gedeon wouldn't have hesitated to crush the competition, literally. Lancelot Lakeland is a waverer. You know what you have to do, and yet you're hesitating. That's not the path to happiness. If you want the girl, take the girl."

Lance shook his head. "That's not the way I want it to be. It has to be her choice. She has to come to me."

Gwenn smiled. "Are you sure she's the right girl for you? I hesitate to bring this up, dear, but it seems to me that your age difference alone is an insurmountable obstacle, even though you don't look a day over four hundred." Gwenn's eyes scanned his body, and she ran her hand across his abs. "But a well-preserved four hundred."

Lance's face registered alarm.

"Don't worry. But you do look good enough to eat."

"Don't get any ideas."

"You're no fun at all."

"Are you here to help me or to hunt me?"

"To help you, of course."

"Well, Aurora Dawn is on her way over."

"She was just here. Can't get enough of you?"

"She's worried about the missing boy. He's a family friend. I think she's just looking for comfort."

"Well, you be sure and give it to her."

Lance squeezed the stuffed toy and scowled. "If you did take the boy, you need to put him back."

"Now how would I go about doing that, if I had him?"

"The same way you plucked him out of his bed, out of his house, and away from his family."

"You ask the impossible." Gwenn swept out of the room and down the basement stairs.

"Where are you going?"

"I have some things to take care of."

"In the basement?"

"Basements can be a refuge."

Lance looked puzzled. Then the doorbell rang. He hurried to the door.

"Aurora Dawn," he said, his breath coming in rapid beats. "It's so nice to see you again." He gathered her into his arms, smelled her sweetness, and nuzzled her neck. Her spirit shone brightly against the night. "Did you miss me?"

Aurora Dawn looked up at Lance. "Yes, as a matter of fact, I did."

"You sound frightened."

"The kidnapping of the boy, Trent, a boy I used to babysit for—it threw me. There could be a killer on the loose in this neighborhood. You don't know where he's going to strike next."

"Or she."

"Why do you say that?"

"Maybe it's an equal opportunity kidnapper."

"Lance, don't even joke about a thing like this."

"Don't worry. You're safe with me. You have nothing to be afraid of. Let's sit down." Aurora Dawn detangled herself from his embrace, and they sat down on the couch.

"My mother thinks that maybe he wandered off from his house to explore the new house on the block. *Your* house."

Lance shifted uncomfortably. "This late at night? How old did you say the boy was?"

"I didn't, but he's thirteen."

Lance had hidden the stuffed rabbit behind a couch pillow.

Aurora Dawn reached over to the same place now, asking, "Is this a sock… It's Mr. Bunny! What is Mr. Bunny doing in your living room?"

"Mr. Bunny?" Lance asked innocently.

"When I babysat for the Baders, Trent never went anywhere without that rabbit. He'd pitch a fit if he couldn't find it."

"I don't know what that thing is doing here. It was here when we moved in. I was just tidying up."

"I need to call my father and let him know. That's an important clue. My mother was right. Trent must have been in this house."

Aurora reached for her phone in her pocket. Lance grabbed her arm.

"I don't think that's such a good idea."

"Lance, what is going on here? What are you hiding? Are you keeping a secret from me?"

"I wouldn't do that. If this is the boy's rabbit, he must have been here looking around. But he's obviously not here anymore."

Aurora Dawn smiled nervously. "Lance, I haven't had a tour of the house. Could you show me around?"

Lance got up from the couch and pulled Aurora Dawn along with him.

"Let's start in my bedroom."

"I'd rather start in the basement."

"The basement? Whatever for?"

"It's just a feeling I have."

"Are you a psychic like your mother?"

"Would that be a problem?"

"Not for me. Are you really a psychic?"

"Not by profession, but yes, and I come by it honestly. My grandmother was also a psychic."

"Double whammy."

"Yes, well some it, a lot of it, actually, rubbed off."

Lance rubbed Aurora Dawn's breasts. "Where exactly did it rub off? Here?" Then he moved his hands to her stomach. "Or here?" Then lower to cup her behind. "Or perhaps, here?"

"Lance, stop it. Don't distract me. I need to know if Trent was in this house. Let's start with the basement."

"Um, this is embarrassing. My parents are down there, having a bit of a lie-in."

"In the basement?"

"Well, my parents are very demonstrative. I mean they don't have to be in bed to, well, you know. I think they want to christen all the rooms."

Aurora Dawn wrinkled her nose. "Yuck."

"You see why I don't think it would be a good idea to go down there. As a matter of fact, why don't we go up to my bedroom and see if the springs are working."

"Lance…"

"You came over, Aurora Dawn. I guess I got the idea that you wanted to see me."

"I did. I do."

"Well, then let's go up to my room and work our way down to the basement. Give the lovebirds some time to finish up."

Lance and Aurora Dawn walked up the stairs hand in hand. He led her into his bedroom.

She walked over to the window. "Is this where you first saw me?"

Lance smiled. "I saw you in my dreams, long before I actually met you, but yes, here's where I first saw you let your hair down, so to speak. Your Rapunzel routine. Do you do that often?"

"Every day, and nothing happened until you moved next door."

"We were meant to be together. I'm sure of it."

"Do you believe in fate?"

"Absolutely."

"I do, too. I've been waiting for someone…for you, I think."

Lancelot took Aurora Dawn in his arms and held her. "And I've been waiting for you for a longer time than you can imagine." He took possession of her lips, feeding on them as she clung to him.

"Lance," she sighed desperately.

"I'm right here," he answered, deepening his kiss while he moved her toward his bed.

"Lance, I don't think—"

"Then don't think. Just feel." He threw his body onto the bed and pulled her on top of him.

Aurora Dawn expelled a breath. She was burning with a fever. She craved Lance. Wanted his hands and mouth on her breasts. She was vibrating. Or was that her phone? She pulled it out of the pocket of her jeans.

"Don't answer it," Lance murmured.

"It's my mother. It might be about the case." Aurora Dawn punched the button.

"Mom," she answered breathlessly.

"Are you okay? You sound out of breath."

"I'm okay. Is there news about Trent?"

"You're not going to believe it, but he's back. He's back in his bed, sleeping soundly, as if he had never left."

"But that doesn't make any sense."

"No, it doesn't. The police want to question him, but he's out like a light."

"But how did the kidnappers get him back up to his room with the police there?"

"I don't know. It's a miracle."

Aurora Dawn whispered in Lance's ear. "Trent is home safe."

Lance breathed a sigh of relief.

"But how?" she asked her mother.

"His parents are so happy to have him home, they don't care."

"I'm so glad to hear that. What about Mr. Bunny?"

"He's nowhere to be found. Come home now."

Aurora Dawn looked at Lancelot and gripped the phone. "I'll be right there."

Chapter Thirteen

"I'm so relieved Trent is back," Aurora Dawn sighed, squeezing Kate's hand.

"So am I," Jack said. "But I'm afraid we have a bigger problem. I just got a call from the Midtown precinct. Another little boy is missing. From a nearby neighborhood. I'm afraid we may have a serial situation."

"Dad, no!" Aurora Dawn's mind went back to Mr. Bunny. She'd left the rabbit at Lance's house. She should tell her father about the stuffed toy. But she didn't want to implicate Lance.

"I'm needed down at the precinct. They're setting up a task force. One kidnapping in Buckhead was an exception. Two is beyond a coincidence."

"Jack, surely they can find someone else. Our daughter is getting married the day after tomorrow. You're needed here."

"What about the parents of the missing boy? I can't abandon them. Kate, this is my case, our case."

"I know you feel an obligation. But the city has enough manpower to handle it. Can we, just for once, not get involved?"

Jack faced Kate and grasped her hands. "They need us. I need you. Will you help me?"

"We have about a million things to do before the ceremony."

"Kate, please."

Kate blew out a breath. "Okay, I'll see if I can come up with anything. You say the child was taken from our neighborhood?"

"Yes, in a house on Paces Ferry Drive."

"Same security setup?"

"Yes," Jack answered. "The boy was taken from his upstairs bedroom. No alarms were set off."

"I'm beginning to see a pattern," Kate observed.

Aurora Dawn paced the room.

"Sweetheart, why don't you try to get some sleep? Your father and I will handle this. You need your rest. You have a big weekend coming up."

Aurora Dawn was anxious to leave her parents. She needed to talk to Lance.

She went up to her bedroom and looked across the lawn. Lance's bedroom light was still on. The briars were beginning to thicken around the house next door. The lawn company had just finished clearing the trees and the thicket, but the underbrush was reappearing at a sorcerer's speed.

Aurora Dawn pressed Lance's number on her cell phone.

"Aurora Dawn," Lance answered.

"Hello, Lance."

"Is everything okay?"

Aurora Dawn paused. "No, it is most definitely *not* okay. Another boy went missing, in this neighborhood. Do you know anything about it?"

"Why would you think that?"

"Because Mr. Bunny was in your house. Quite a coincidence, don't you think? And I don't believe in coincidences."

"I explained that. Just a boy looking for adventure around an empty house."

"My father is working the case. If you know anything, you'd better tell me."

Lance's body stiffened against the window.

"Come to me, Aurora Dawn," he said.

"Lance, I'm getting married in two days. I am not leaving the house again tonight. But if you have any information about the missing boy, please contact my father." She gave Lance her father's private number and severed the phone connection.

Chapter Fourteen

Jack Hale was more than surprised to receive Lance Lakeland's phone call. But here he was, sitting in Jack's study, offering to help find another missing boy. All Jack could think about was Aurora Dawn and how this man was going to ruin his daughter's future. He couldn't let that happen. He couldn't be sure who this Lancelot person was, or if he was who he claimed to be. Or if he was a supernatural being, from another world—a vampire? Was that even possible? Well, for his daughter's sake, he was going to get to the bottom of the mystery. Just come right out and accuse him and gauge his reaction.

"I'm giving you a chance to come clean. I know you're not Lancelot Lakeland. Lancelot Lakeland does not exist, except in some secret WITSEC database. What I want to know, demand to know, is who are you and what do you want with my daughter? Does the name Gedeon Nagy ring a bell?"

Lance stammered some nonsensical answer, looked down at his feet, and fidgeted, giving Jack all the information he needed to know.

"H-how did you know?"

"Never mind how I know. Now, I want some answers, young man. How old are you anyway?"

Lance greeted Aurora Dawn's father with silence.

"What can you offer my daughter? A lifetime of

pain and regret? You're a monster. The things you've done, if I am to believe you are this Gedeon person or thing, make you all wrong for Aurora Dawn. I can't even wrap my head around what you are. I won't allow it. She's walking into this relationship blindly. So either you tell her the truth or I will. I will not let you ruin her life."

Lance rubbed his hand across his mouth. "Here's what I will promise you, sir. I will try to be a good man. All that I have and all that I am I will give to her. But if you are still against us, I will walk away. That's how much I love her. I have sacrificed future lifetimes for her."

"Can you go back—to where you came from, to what you were?" Jack asked. "Somewhere far away from here?"

"I would not want to. I cannot deny I've done some unforgiveable things. But I am not that person anymore. I've been waiting for Aurora Dawn my whole life. She is the other half of my soul. I don't want to be with another woman."

"I've read your journals. You've wanted Juliette, and her mother before that, and your first love, Marika. I'm no psychiatrist, but I think you're confused about what you want and who you want."

"I *was* confused. Now I'm sure of who and what I want. I want your daughter. And I want to help you solve your case."

Jack took a good look at Lancelot Lakeland—or Gedeon Nagy, or whatever his name was. He looked repentant, but was he sincere?

"What makes you think you could help this investigation, or that I'd even want your help?"

"I am—I was—a stalker, Mr. Hale. I know how these people think. I can help you find this boy. I want to offer my assistance."

Jack grimaced. He could use all the help he could get, but he'd be damned if he'd take help from this creature. But a young boy was in jeopardy. Who knew who had him or what nefarious things they were planning? He was desperate. Desperate enough to accept help from any quarter.

Lance offered his hand. Jack swallowed his pride and shook it, hoping he wouldn't regret it.

If they were going to work together, he would take the measure of this man or beast or creature or whoever the hell was standing before him. The man his daughter appeared to love.

Chapter Fifteen

Lance paced the length of the foyer like a caged panther. He turned toward the staircase and shouted, "Gwenn, get down here."

Gwenn surfaced on the stairwell, held the banister, and wound her way down the stairs.

"Where's the king?" Lance demanded.

"The king?"

"King Arthur, or whatever his real name is. Your husband."

"He's indisposed at the moment, with a little project down in the basement."

Lance grabbed Gwenn's arm and pulled her down onto the couch.

"Okay, I want answers now. There's another young boy missing. Don't bother lying to me. Did you take him?"

Gwenn looked properly affronted.

"You specifically told me not to hunt in the neighborhood."

"Don't play word games with me. This boy was taken from his home just a few miles away."

"But not in our neighborhood?" Gwenn posed. "That was our agreement."

"When I said no hunting in the neighborhood, I didn't mean that literally. I didn't mean that you should satisfy your cravings in the next neighborhood. I meant no hunting anywhere near here. And preferably not in the next county or even the next state, and certainly someone more age appropriate."

"Why didn't you say what you meant, then?"

"It's a disgusting habit, *Mother,* and I won't tolerate it. Why don't you stick to deer?"

Gwenn laughed. "Deer are so boring. They offer no resistance. Apparently, you have a short memory. It wasn't that long ago when you had to satisfy your blood cravings, and you weren't that particular about who you drained or where. Or have you forgotten?"

Lance sprang from the couch and turned back to face her. "I've forgotten nothing. But you're complicating an already complicated situation. You can't keep snatching children from their bedrooms in the middle of the night. Now, I insist you return that boy to his parents immediately."

Gwenn laughed. "Darling, I know you're not threatening me. You are not exactly coming from a position of power. Gedeon the Devastator is not so devastating anymore."

Lance grabbed her by the shoulders. "I wouldn't be so sure of that. I don't know what my powers are. You don't want to test me. I'll call Count Nagy."

Gwenn twisted out of Lance's grasp and headed for the basement.

"You and Art have been spending an awfully long time in the basement lately. Is that where you have the boy?"

Gwenn turned around to face Lance and pouted. "No need to call the count. I will make the situation right."

"I'm coming down to the basement. Do you have

him restrained, or have you glamoured him?"

Gwenn raised her hand to stop him. "I haven't said the boy was in the house. Think for a minute, before you expose yourself. You can't afford to be involved if you want to protect your precious reputation and have any chance with the girl. We will handle it."

Lance fumed. "If you've hurt the boy, I swear I'll—"

"Don't be so dramatic. We've taken a few little practice nips. Haven't even broken the skin—yet. Relax. Invite your little girlfriend over and release some of that pent-up energy you seem to be storing. Sex does wonders for a hot temper."

"Leave Aurora Dawn out of this. She's off limits."

Gwenn licked her lips. "That's a shame. She would make a tender little morsel. Your father has developed quite an appetite for goodness and light."

Lance folded his arms and fumed, first as Gwenn descended into the basement, then while his parents busied themselves downstairs before they left the house. If he only had his powers, he would make short work of the imposters. This Knights of the Round Table business had gone too far. The idea of his "parents" being named after Queen Guinevere and King Arthur was preposterous. And Lancelot? The Arthurian legend was just mythology dating back to the fifth or sixth century. Way before his time. Even though Gwenn and Art insisted they used to be acquainted with the real King Arthur. He had a feeling they were beginning to believe their own fantasy.

Lance's heart galloped. His blood began to boil. He took a deep breath in an attempt to curb his temper and crush all prior thoughts of his bad behavior. His hunting days were over. After all, he was a human being. A reasonable human being. And he was working hard to become the best man he could be. Lancelot Lakeland.

Lance paced until he heard his parents reenter the house. He let an appropriate amount of time pass before he picked up his cell phone and placed a call to Jack Hale.

"Everything will be okay, Mr. Hale. The ordeal will soon be over. You will find the missing boy, and you can put this all behind you."

"The parents are frantic. This has to stop. Do you know something?"

"It's just a strong feeling I have."

"You sound like my wife and my mother-in-law—and my daughter, for that matter."

"I'm sure you will be getting some good news soon."

Lance hung up the phone and rubbed his neck. He wanted Aurora Dawn, and he wanted her right now. In fact, he could hardly control his cravings. He needed her. He flexed his hands and dialed her number.

"Aurora Dawn," he began when she answered the phone. "I need to see you right away."

"Lance, the best news. They found the second little boy."

Lance breathed a sigh of relief.

"Was he hurt?"

"Just frightened, a little bruised, but he has no memory of what happened to him. He's home safe with his family. My father said you were very calm under pressure. He had some good things to say about the way you handled yourself. He was very impressed. He thinks you might have a future as a psychic detective."

Lance rubbed his chin. He had his hands full trying to curb his "parents'" baser tendencies. The last thing he needed was to get involved with Aurora Dawn's parents. And he needed to advance his plan to win his lady's heart. There wasn't much time left.

"How soon can you get here?" Lance said impatiently.

"I'm on my way."

Chapter Sixteen

When Aurora Dawn arrived at the Stryer mansion, Lance took her trembling hands in his at the front door.

"Now that we're in this 'burning ring of fire,' what are we going to do about it?" Lance growled.

Aurora Dawn moved into his arms. He carried her into the keeping room, where they settled comfortably, relaxing and snuggling on the couch, as close as two people could get. Their time together was bittersweet and precious. Aurora Dawn realized this might be one of the last opportunities she and Lance would have to be alone together.

"What are your dreams for the future, my love? Do they lean in the psychic direction? Are you going to follow in your parents' footsteps and go into the family business solving crimes?"

Aurora Dawn contemplated the question before she spoke.

"My grandfather is about to retire, and I'm sure my father could use my talents in his agency, but I'm not interested at all in tracking down serial killers or monetizing my psychic abilities. My mother has done that, and she's paid a heavy price. She won't admit it, but I know it bothers her. She lives with evil, and it's invading her spirit. But I do have dreams, daydreams, really. I've been working on a book...about vampires. About one benevolent vampire in particular, if you believe in those. A vampire with a pure heart."

Lance sat up, alert, his arm still around Aurora Dawn. "Vampires? Whatever gave you that idea?" He hoped to God that Jack Hale hadn't told his daughter about his true identity before he had a chance to tell her himself.

"It's a fairytale my grandmother used to tell me about a beautiful Romani and a powerful vampire. In her story, the vampire was evil, and the story didn't have a happy ending, but the vampire truly loved the woman, in his own way. It got me to thinking. What if there was such a thing as a good vampire?"

Lance cocked his head and stared into Aurora Dawn's eyes. "Do you believe that is possible?"

"Are you asking if I believe in the existence of vampires, or if I believe a vampire could be good?"

"Both."

"My grandmother believes that anything is possible. She's seen some strange and amazing things in her life. She thinks we should be open to everything. She's a very wise woman."

Lance banded his body to Aurora Dawn's. He hungered to tell her the truth. But he didn't have the words. Spinning imaginary vampire tales was one thing. Being confronted with a real-life vampire in the flesh—a vampire with evil inclinations but the best intentions—was entirely another. If he told her the truth, she'd go running. He would never hold her in his arms again, never kiss her, never know the quiet contentment he had found whenever she was around. He'd waited a lifetime for her. She filled a gaping hole in his long but meaningless existence, and he couldn't even contemplate living without her. Could he be that selfish?

They had never discussed marriage, not in so many words, not with her imminent marriage looming like a monstrous shadow on the landscape of their love. But he owed her honesty. He decided to step off the precipice. If she truly loved him, then anything was possible.

"Aurora Dawn. I want to marry you. Will you be my wife?"

Aurora Dawn broke away from Lance and smiled in anticipation and with joy.

"To be yours, my darling Lance, in every way." Aurora Dawn took a deep breath. "Is that even possible now?"

"If you wish it, then anything is possible. My fate is entirely in your hands."

Lance fingered the sparkling emerald ring on his right hand. It was an heirloom given to him by his Maker. Its value was beyond price. He'd sworn never to take it off. If he shopped for a ring today in the most exclusive store, he couldn't find its match. He loosened the ring, and it slid right off.

"I would give you this as my promise to seal our love. I promise to love you forever or for whatever time we have."

Aurora Dawn grasped the ring in her hand, then openly admired it. "Oh, Lance, it's absolutely beautiful."

"Not nearly as beautiful as you are."

Aurora Dawn smiled shyly, mesmerized by the hypnotic power of the pale green stone in the vintage setting.

"I'm glad you like it. But I'm anxious to hear your

answer."

Aurora Dawn handed the ring back to Lance. "If I weren't getting married tomorrow, my answer would be yes, of course, yes. Put the ring on my finger, if only for a moment."

Lance lifted Aurora Dawn's finger and placed the ring on it. "Now, we're betrothed."

"For tonight, anyway."

"Then let's make tonight last."

It would be so easy to caress her, kiss her, love her. He frowned, his conscience pricking at the perimeter of his thoughts. Apparently, he did have a conscience. "But before you give me your answer, there's something I want you to read."

Lance handed Aurora Dawn a sheaf of yellowing pages. He'd promised her father he would reveal his true identity, and, more than anything, he wanted to be a man of his word.

"What is this?" Aurora Dawn took the pile of papers and sat down on the couch.

"Just read it. It will soon become clear."

Aurora Dawn took the pages from Lance and settled back to begin reading while Lance proceeded to pace the length of the room. At some passages she nodded, lost in the fabric of the story. At some, her eyebrows shot up, and Lance could hear her intake of breath and see a hand fly to her heart.

"Who is this Gedeon? Is he a relative? Is that why you have his chronicles?"

Lance held her gaze. "Can't you guess the answer?"

Aurora Dawn shook her head in denial. "Y-you're not saying that you're…you're G-Gedeon? How is that possible? You would have to be, I mean, how old are you?"

"You see the date on the journals."

"1625?" she whispered. "Is this some kind of a joke?"

"It's not a joke. You need to read the rest of what's written. Read it now."

Aurora Dawn continued reading.

The Nagy Chronicles 1625—

I met the count before he had his own sons, who later became princes, while he was head of a minor noble family in the northern part of the kingdom of Hungary. He was dashing and brash, and I was a young, impressionable soldier in his charge. It didn't matter that I was about to marry Marika, a girl I had been in love with since childhood. A girl who swore her love to me.

The count had his eye on me, and one night, after a particularly bloody battle and an even sweeter victory, when we were both exhausted and I was under the influence of too much wine, he professed his feelings. I thought of Marika, but the count and I were brothers-in-arms. We had sworn to die for each other.

That night, what followed seemed a most natural course of action. In return for my body and my lifelong loyalty, he offered me his love, his protection, his family name, his wealth, a title, and the gift of immortality. When he put his mark on me, he was my first, for Marika and I had not yet lain together. And although I never would have imagined wanting what we had together, it was a glorious night. A night I will always remember. The first of many such nights. And indeed, I did love him, first in the way a soldier loves his commander, but then in a more intimate and intense way. A carnal love, born of lust. A blood bond. And that love changed me.

After that, I was no longer the man Marika fell in love with, and I had to turn away from her, for her own protection. She was shocked and shattered. Eventually, she married someone else, and I moved in with the count, in his castle on the mountain. I never stopped loving Marika, and sometimes, in the middle of the night, I would come down from the castle to visit her. She never knew I was there, or that I had to live with the pain of watching her with another man—her husband with his hands all over her, caressing her, seducing her with his lips, and the two of them with their new family—their beautiful daughters—and I continued to watch her, and watch over her, until the day she died. I cried at her grave. Marika was my one true love. The love I could never have.

And what of the count, my Maker, the man who initiated me into his secret brood? He went on to marry and start a dynasty, to live in other, richer castles, and he left me in mine. Eventually, we grew apart but for his occasional visits, which always left me wanting more. Wanting more comfort. Missing his company and companionship, and also missing my first true love.

And wondering whether things would have been different if I had stayed with Marika and lived a normal human life. But I was anything but normal. It was an impossible dream.

Aurora Dawn sat transfixed. "This can't be you. I won't believe it. I want to hear it in your own words."

"Those centuries were some of the longest and the loneliest, and I'm afraid I developed some vile habits that make me ashamed," Lance began. "I cavorted with my kind in a number of empty, mind-numbing relationships, and engaged in other liaisons to try to recapture the human love I had with Marika, some by mutual consent and others, yes, often, by force when it suited me and my chosen victim was unwilling."

Aurora Dawn gasped.

"But I am what I am. And there is no going back. In my world, there are no second chances. There was no one I cared to share eternity with. I was known by many names through many lifetimes. But the given name Gedeon caught my fancy. The Devastator. So that identity stuck. For my family name, I kept the name of my noble sire, Nagy, which in Hungarian means a large and powerful person. Read on. I want you to know everything."

1945—

By the end of World War II, during which many of the royal landowners were displaced, jailed or deported, I had joined the Arrow Cross, a Hungarian Fascist movement, aligned with the German Nazis, that seized power in 1944. At first, it was just a diversion, but it turned out to be a wise decision, since my castle and all surrounding lands were spared from the vagaries of war. And then I began to enjoy the night forays into Budapest. We would roam the streets in our green uniforms and badges—a set of crossed arrows— and rob, terrorize, and slaughter the unfortunate locals.

My home was a fortress, so the castle was the ideal storage depot for the Nazis' stolen loot, as were the salt mines, cellars, convents, and other safe houses that had been earmarked by the Reich. And when the Soviet troops drove the Nazis out of Hungary, they left behind vast stores of treasures—diamonds, thousands of sculptures, paintings, watercolors, furniture, and other priceless art and antiquities looted and seized from homes and museums throughout Europe. No one knew about my secret cache, and because I had enough money to pay off the Soviets, my castle and all my holdings were spared. I was a survivor, in the strictest sense of the word.

I became a patron of the arts, and I had recovered these precious works of art. Every day, I would enter the storage rooms in the castle and catalog the treasures—landscapes, skylines, and portraits by Van Gogh, Matisse, Degas, Picasso, Chagall, Vermeer. The list was endless, as were the opportunities to unload the masterpieces to "collectors" to finance the upkeep of the castle.

"So when you say you trade in art, you meant *stolen* art," Aurora Dawn stated, almost spitting the last words. "You hoarded works of art or sold them to the highest bidder, so no one else could enjoy their beauty."

Lance nodded.

Aurora Dawn read on.

1983—

I had all the riches in the world but no one to share them with. There were many women, of course, and men, over the years. I had needs, after all. But none captured my heart or heated my blood like my Marika, my first love. So when I first laid eyes on a beautiful Romani woman camped outside my castle, I knew she was the incarnation of Marika and that, by some great miracle, she had returned to me. She was the image of Marika, right down to her beckoning violet eyes and coal-black hair. I had to make this woman mine. She didn't know me or what we had shared together, so she was shy at first. How could I tell her we had met in another lifetime? What we had meant to each other? Where could I find the words? How could I tell her we were destined to be together? How could I explain a lifetime of yearning? I didn't want to scare her away. So, even though I was impatient to bed her, I courted her until she seemed to develop genuine feelings for me.

I vowed to be her protector, and, with a young daughter to feed and no means of support, at first she was receptive when I wooed her. She said another man—a prince from a faraway land—had made similar promises and did nothing to protect her when his wife sent her and her child away. I was jealous of that man, but I held my temper. Instead, I gave her gifts and treasures and spoke to her of my love. I even had her portrait painted—a portrait of Marika and her daughter—so I could look upon her beauty anytime I pleased. And I was happy with her, until one day she noticed my eyes wandering to Ilona—her daughter was growing more lovely and ripe each day. And I wanted to taste her, just a sample, for she reminded me of a younger Marika, and I desired her. My lady pulled away from me because she didn't understand my hunger and my needs. But she knew I was powerful, and that I would get my way eventually, and that nothing she could say would stop me. She agreed to marry me if I would leave her daughter alone. I was delirious with joy. Finally, I would be reunited with my true love. But all those centuries of corruption made it impossible for me to resist the temptation, impossible for me to be denied. I sent my guards to pick up Ilona and bring her to me for a closer inspection. I told them to tell her mother I only wanted to make the child feel welcome in our home, that I had a special dress I wanted her to wear to the wedding, and a special room picked out just for her in the castle, close to our bedroom. There were preparations to be made, and I wanted her to be a part of them. I paced my bedroom, stroking my beard and rubbing my thumb across my bottom lip in anticipation of my juicy pre-wedding appetizer.

Aurora Dawn felt the bile rise in her throat as she forced herself to continue.

The guards marched down the hill, and when they returned empty-handed, reporting the child had vanished, I'm afraid I lost my temper, and Marika paid the price. I thought Marika would come around, eventually, and tell me where the child was, but no amount of torture or pain or starvation made a dent in her defiance and, one day, when I had her brought to my bedroom, it was her body I held, but her spirit had already left this earth, before I could make her mine forever. I thought we were going to share everything. But my true love was gone from me again. And I vowed that if I ever found Ilona, I would put my brand on her so I wouldn't have to face eternity alone.

I spent countless restless nights and countless florints searching for Ilona. I hunted her down in the dark throughout Europe and all over the world, but I never found her. It was almost as if she had disappeared from the face of the earth, without a trace. No doubt her mother had woven a protective spell over her daughter, shielding her from my sight. For Marika had powerful magic, which she undoubtedly passed on to her daughter. I'd lost Marika, and without Ilona to replace her, I knew I would never be content. I would

never be at peace. So I continued to search...
****

Aurora Dawn's shocked expression wounded him to the core.

"Why didn't you tell me?" Aurora Dawn grabbed the bottom of her T-shirt and bunched it in her fist. Her breathing came in shallow bursts.

"How could I? Where could I start? You wouldn't have believed me anyway."

"I believed *in* you. But now I don't know what to believe." Aurora Dawn hesitated. "I have a million questions."

"You can ask me anything."

"Who was Ilona?"

"Can't you guess? She was your grandmother, Juliette. I tracked her down and took her and—well, you can read for yourself. Your father and your grandfather came to her rescue, and I paid the ultimate price."

"And this Count Nagy. Where is he now? Are you still involved with him?"

Lance pursed his lips. How to explain to a mortal about a Maker? He owed everything to Zoltan Nagy. They weren't together, but he'd be lying if he didn't admit that he didn't still love his Maker in some inexplicable way. He didn't have an answer.

"This man, the man in these diaries, who would do these terrible things, this doesn't sound at all like you."

"I've made mistakes over a long lifetime. I'd be the first to admit that."

"Are you really—but how can you be—are you truly a...vampire?"

"I'm not sure what I am anymore. Once I was a

man. Then I was a vampire. I've been told I'm now back to being mortal."

Aurora Dawn rubbed her hand across her face, her mind deep in thought.

"If we were together…could we have children?"

"Honestly, I don't know. You could, I'm sure, but us together? I may be too broken."

Aurora Dawn stood up suddenly and wobbled on her feet, overcome by dizziness, the papers scattering to the floor. Lance caught her by the hand. She shook him off. More and more, Bronx seemed a much safer prospect. This wasn't a fantasy. This was a horror show beyond imagination. The things this man had done to her great-grandmother and thought about doing to her grandmother—would have done, if Juliette hadn't escaped—made him irredeemable. And he coveted Juliette again, and kidnapped her in Bermuda, with the evilest of intentions. She rubbed her throbbing eyes and her aching forehead. Her immediate inclination was to run. To escape from this haunted nightmare. Nothing was as it seemed. Was this Gedeon person engaged in a plot to snare another innocent girl who reminded him of Marika? Was she just the latest in a long line of poor substitutes? Would he ever get over his long-lost first love? If she were to take a risk with Lance, what would their life be like?

"T-thank you for showing me your journals. I h-have to go. I'm n-needed at home."

Lance grabbed her shoulders and pulled her toward him. "You're needed here. If you have any other questions, all you need to do is ask."

"The questions I have, you have no answers for. Lance, or Gedeon, or whoever you really are, this isn't going to work."

Aurora Dawn turned and walked out the door.

"Aurora Dawn!" Lance pleaded. "Come back, please! Let me explain."

She was right to run away from him. Who he was defied explanation.

****

The house echoed with raw loneliness. Roared with the absence of Aurora Dawn's glorious presence. He had laid his life out before her, and he didn't need extraordinary powers to gauge that his lady love had essentially pushed a stake through his black heart as she backed away, literally *and* figuratively.

His inclination was to go after her. But she needed time. Time to take it all in. To absorb the magnitude of her situation. But time was running out. The wedding was tomorrow. Would he ever see her again? He had to make his move soon. But he was out of options. How could he explain what had happened to him if he didn't understand it himself?

Lance lay prostate on the couch in the keeping room, one arm flung over his face in despair, replaying the scenario in his mind. Going back to the last time he'd been with Zoltan. Trying to make sense out of what had happened to him after his near-death experience on the yacht in Bermuda. An experienced that changed him forever.

****

Groggy and disoriented, Lance, folded in the arms of his Maker, looked up at Count Zoltan Nagy. His Maker's hand rested tenderly on Lance's brow. What was he doing here?

The count's mesmerizing voice poured from his

lips. "Welcome back, Gedeon. We thought we'd lost you."

"What happened to me? I remember—" Lance pressed the back of his hand against his forehead. "It hurts to remember."

"Hush, don't talk," the count whispered. "You were completely shattered. Harder to put back together than Humpty Dumpty. It was touch-and-go there for a while. We had to place you in a deep therapeutic trance sleep. You needed that time to heal."

"How long was I out?"

"More than two decades."

"Incredible. Where have I been?"

"Here, with me. You spent many years in a sanatorium for repair."

"How badly was I hurt?"

"We don't exactly know. How do you feel?"

"Lighter."

"I was afraid of that. What do you remember?"

"I remember you and Marika."

"Not Marika. She's long in the grave, Gedeon. You are remembering that delicious Romani tidbit you played with, then killed, and her daughter Ilona, who calls herself Psychic Juliette. You keep confusing them with Marika. You confuse every woman with Marika."

Lance shrank back into the count's comforting arms. "I loved her."

"You loved her to death. You didn't know your own power. You don't remember how you tortured the poor woman?"

"I wouldn't do that."

"I'm afraid you're suffering from selective memory. Then you became interested in her daughter,

Ilona. Your lover died protecting her daughter."

"Ilona." Lance repeated the name. His mind was numb. "Have I changed?"

"That's what we're trying to determine. No one has ever survived what you went through."

The count handed Lance a mirror.

Lance glanced into the glass and pressed a finger across his brow. "My eyebrow, where is it?"

The count laughed. "Singed when you were almost incinerated on the deck of that boat in Bermuda."

"Will it grow back?"

"It hasn't done in more than twenty years, so I highly doubt it. You're still a handsome devil, with one sexy-looking blonde eyebrow. You look exactly like you looked when I took you in."

Lance frowned. "Why am I here? I thought you had abandoned me."

"You're confused. I had to leave you centuries ago to marry and start my dynasty, but I'd never completely abandon you. I had to call in a lot of favors to save you. I'm here to help you through this difficult transition."

"But you were gone for so long."

"I'll always be here for you, don't you know that?"

In the darkness, the spark of life flared and pulsed. Feeling returned to Lance's lower body, and he angled toward his Maker, all other thoughts pushed aside.

The count could hardly control his laughter. "There will be plenty of time for that. We have much to catch up on, my friend. The castle—"

"What about it?"

Count Nagy had made a mental flyby of Gedeon's former castle in Hungary, the castle he had ceded to his friend, and found everything had changed. The property no longer belonged to Gedeon. His cache of valuable masterpieces was gone. Gedeon would have to find another place to go, another source of income. Another refuge. But this was not the time to discuss that loss.

"I'll provide for you, my beloved," assured the count, his lips slowly dancing up Gedeon's neck in the old way, the way that brought back pleasant memories. "That's all you need to know."

Lance shivered. He hoped this repair would be a smooth one. His mind moved back in time, crawling at a snail's pace. He would have traded all of this for a regular lifetime with Marika. Centuries after she was lost to him, the Romani—or was it her daughter, who now called herself Juliette—had awakened his lust. He was drawn to her, and he would most assuredly have her later, later when he was stronger.

But in his scrying mirror, Count Nagy offered him an incentive to heal faster—the vision of a new woman—Juliette's granddaughter, *Aurora Dawn Hale*. She was so lifelike, he could almost inhale a whiff of her honeyed sweetness. The next generation. Daughter and granddaughter of gifted psychics and great-granddaughter of his delightful Romani lover, whose body he had taken and whose spirit he had crushed. Except for her honey-blonde locks, Aurora Dawn was made in Marika's image. Her life flew by before his eyes. Aurora Dawn as an infant in her grandmother's arms, playing with Juliette's amethyst amulet. The young but alluring Aurora Dawn in pigtails, hints of delicious curves even then. Aurora Dawn and some young buck at her high school prom. Her college years. She had grown more beautiful and regal each day and now she was ready to walk down the aisle with that same man.

"I am showing you these visions because this girl is your destiny," the count announced. "She was ordained for you. Marika's blood runs in her veins. She is truly the incarnation of your lost love. She's the one you've been pining for, waiting for, all these years."

Lance's heart heated, then simmered to a slow boil. Count Nagy pulled back the mirror.

Lance railed, reaching out. "Just one more look at my beloved."

"First things first," the count said. "You need to finish healing." He faced Lance. "I know you went back to visit Marika when we were first together. And that you continued to visit her after she was married."

"She had no idea I was observing her." Lance hung his head. "I didn't know you knew."

"There isn't much I don't know about you, Gedeon. I know your heart, and it still belongs to Marika, after all these centuries."

Lance nodded in acknowledgement. But Marika was lost to him forever. Aurora Dawn offered him new hope. He would have to wait for her. But didn't he have a lifetime to wait? Two lifetimes? As many lifetimes as he wanted?

As if reading his innermost thoughts, Zoltan spoke.

"Would you like to see your love, Ilona's granddaughter, the one you've had your eye on since she was a baby? She's all grown up."

His next vision, courtesy of the count, was a premonition. Aurora Dawn Hale appeared as a fully-blossomed woman, ravishing and virginal in bridal white. She was ready to march down the aisle, but she was not eager to wed and bed her young man. They hadn't been together as a man and a woman, yet. But the young man was panting for her. Well, dammit all, so was he.

As the count offered up repeated visions of Aurora Dawn, Lance was drawn to her, as he was to no other woman, and he would have her, later, when he was on the mend. He would find a way to taste her and tap into her glorious goodness and light before any other man, heaven forbid, feasted on her and captured her power.

"Do you suppose, after my restoration, I could be g—good?" Lance stuttered, his face turned up toward the count, the sun, the moon, and the stars in his heaven.

The count bellowed, almost choking on his laughter. "At least you haven't lost your sense of humor."

"But maybe she would love me, if only…"

The count put his hand on Lance's shoulder. "In truth, you are the bravest and truest soul I know. You're entirely worthy. You lost your way after you lost Marika. And that is almost entirely my fault. Now is your chance to fix what's broken inside you."

Count Nagy observed his progeny's vision as if it were displayed on a video screen. "She is a stunning creature. You have the power to make her love you with or without her consent. You know that. Or you used to."

"But if she's like all the other women in her family, she can sense evil. She'll sense my presence and be repelled."

"You are superior to her, a mere mortal woman, in every way. But, my love, no thoughts of another woman tonight. It's been centuries since I touched you, and I grow impatient for your body."

Lance groaned and reached for his Maker out of habit, all thoughts of goodness and light flying out of his head.

"You're weak, like a baby lamb, but I will be gentle. Come, let me love you."

Gedeon the Devastator—that's what they used to call him—tried to fight the twisted evil inside of him. He consented to let the count make love to him in the old way. But he couldn't erase his yearning for Aurora Dawn, the new pink flesh, the curvaceous body, the angelic face, the soul as fresh as a newly laundered sheet. He needed her to make his restoration complete. Mixing the good with the bad, that was always the way.

Now their moment was almost at hand.

When the count's hunger was slaked, he spoke to Lance, who lay spent in his arms, about the way things would play out.

"I've sensed your mounting desire for this girl, and I've set you up in the house next door on the pretext that your family is in the witness protection program. Your 'mother and father' will be ours, of course, and they'll be at your service to smooth the way. It's a colorful house with a colorful history in Atlanta—the heart of the Deep South."

Lance snorted. "A family of vampires in the witness protection program? It sounds like the premise for a bad sitcom."

"A clever arrangement, don't you think?"

"That remains to be seen. Why Atlanta? Why not New Orleans?"

"It's easier to stay below the radar in Atlanta. And as they say in the musical, 'Because your love is there.'

Of course, there are conditions."

"What kind of conditions?"

The count hesitated before he spoke. "You'll be giving up a lot for love. Your past, your powers, your immortality. You've exhausted your nine lives, I'm afraid, my friend. In order to bring you back—that is, as a condition of your restoration—you will be like any other mortal."

Lance sniffed the intoxicating aroma of incense in the bedroom and took a whiff of Count Nagy's body. Would he ever get that blasted smell out of his mind?

"That will be a blessing. Living through the centuries without love is not living. I'll look forward to seeing the sun again. But what if she doesn't love me? Won't have me?"

"I guarantee she won't be able to resist you."

Lance frowned. "I don't want to force her."

The count raised his brows. "Well, then you're halfway there. You're almost rehabilitated."

Lance stared into the count's eyes. "Why are you doing this for me?"

The count laughed. "You know the old saying, 'Don't look a fire-breathing gift-dragon in the mouth.' " Then he became quiet before he spoke again.

"Because I owe you," Zoltan admitted. "Penance? Atonement? To right a wrong; to restore what I took from you all those years ago. To reunite your souls. There has to be balance in the universe. She can be yours again. We never forget our first love. Those memories are imprinted on our brains."

"Do you remember your first love?"

"You were my first love. You've served me well, my old friend. You were meant to be with Marika until

I…turned your head. I can't bring her back, but I *can* do this for you. What you do with your life from now on is up to you. Your sins have been washed away. You've been given a clean slate. You will appear as you did when you first met Marika. You were quite handsome, as I recall. You still are. The years have been good to you."

"This time, I intend to make better decisions. Will I see you again?"

"In your dreams, of course, and whenever you wish. But the decision must be yours. If you want to banish me from your life, that is your prerogative. It is all within your power."

Lance disentangled from the count's embrace with some regret.

"Then do what you have to do. I'm anxious to meet my destiny."

Chapter Seventeen

The Day of the Wedding

Aurora Dawn reclined on the couch in the living room of the Crystal Palace, her hand splayed across her forehead, staring into her mother's eyes.

"What do you see when you look into his soul?" Kate asked, lifting the tepid cloth from her daughter's brow.

"I know I should be repulsed, but I only see light and goodness."

"Are you sure you're not seeing your love for him reflected in his eyes?"

"Would that be so bad?"

"Has he shared his history with you?"

"I've read the chronicles."

"Your father told me the story. He is an evil man." Kate had first-hand experience with evil men. She didn't want her daughter to repeat that experience.

"*Was* an evil man," Aurora Dawn insisted.

"Maybe your love is blinding you to the evil inside him. You know what he's done, who he is, the sins he's capable of."

"I know my own heart. I wouldn't love him if he were evil. He's striving to be good."

"How can you say that? You're simply trying to justify his behavior. This is the type of man, this is exactly the man, your father and I have been trying to protect you from."

"I don't know what to think."

"What will you do about Bronx? Does he know what you've been up to?"

"I have to be honest with him. He might not want to marry me after we talk. I'll have to tell him before the wedding."

Kate glanced at her diamond wrist watch. "Which starts in about an hour. You'd better go find him."

"What will you tell the Bambergers if I—?" She left the question unasked.

Kate shrugged. "I'll think of something."

Aurora Dawn hugged her mother. "Thank you for understanding."

"I'm not sure I do. But I will respect your decision. I think, however, that you should march right down the aisle with your childhood friend—even if he is the devil you know."

"Well, thank you for supporting me."

Chapter Eighteen

Aurora Dawn found Bronx in the sunroom of the Crystal Palace, perhaps her favorite room, knocking back a glass of scotch. The fragrant smell of flowers invaded her senses.

"Drinking already?"

"It calms my nerves. The photographer has been looking for you. I told her you were getting dressed."

Aurora Dawn frowned. She was already in her wedding gown, missing only the veil. She was glad they were having an open bar. Bronx was going to need major fortification when she told him the news.

"I thought it was bad luck for the groom to see the bride before the wedding," he announced, his eyes flat.

"Well, actually, it is. But there's not going to be a wedding."

Bronx brought the tumbler down with force. A splash of scotch spread across the glass table like a clear inkblot. He turned to face Aurora Dawn, ready to do battle.

"What?"

"I came to tell you we have to call off the wedding."

Bronx blinked. "What are you saying?"

"I can't marry you, Bronx."

"Why not?" Bronx barked.

"I haven't been completely honest with you."

"What do you mean? You've never lied a day in your life."

"I've fallen in love. With the boy next door."

Bronx's mouth fell open, and he rounded on her. "That sounds like some teeny-bopper love ballad."

"It's not a teeny-bopper love song. I'm in love with someone else."

Bronx expelled a whiskey-tinged breath, barely able to contain himself. "When did this happen? And who is the boy next door?"

"In the last week. He just moved in, and I don't know how, but we fell in love." Aurora Dawn was hesitant to reveal Lance's true identity. That would be more than Bronx could handle.

"Do you know how crazy that sounds? You're leaving me at the altar? You can't do that. *Town & Country* is here. We were going to get the cover. You're already in your wedding gown."

Aurora Dawn folded her arms across her chest. "You're worried about your image. I'm following my heart."

Bronx looked mad enough to tear the gown from her body, yard by lace yard.

"Bronx. Listen to yourself. That's not what's important."

"Why are you doing this?"

"I've been trying to tell you, but you're not listening."

Bronx cleared his throat. "I'm listening now."

"It's like I said. We saw each other, and it was fate. We were meant to be together. I tried to fight it."

"That's romantic rubbish. What is his name? What does he do?"

"His name is Lancelot Lakeland, and he's in the import-export business."

"That sounds sketchy. Import-export could be anything. And what kind of name is Lancelot?"

"He's from Hungary."

Bronx laughed. "Let me understand this. You just met this Lancelot person a week ago, and you're dumping me, someone you've known for years, for some Hungarian horn-dog who would steal someone else's fiancé on his wedding day? What do your parents think about it?"

"They're not happy, but they know I'm in love."

"I thought you were in love with me."

"I love you, of course. But I'm *in love* with Lance. I can't marry him now after what I've learned about his past, but it's not fair of me to marry you when my heart belongs to someone else."

Bronx stood up. "I want to meet this guy."

"He's right next door. Do you want me to take you over there?"

"He lives in the haunted house?"

"It's not haunted, at least, not anymore."

"Aurora Dawn, do you know how crazy this sounds? I'm going over there with or without you."

"I don't want to see him, but I don't want you going over there alone. I'm afraid you'll get hurt."

"Me? Why would I get hurt?"

"He's big."

"How big?"

"Very big. And powerful. You'll see. I don't want you two to fight over me."

"I thought that's what you wanted, two knights-errant battling over the fair maiden. That's always been your naïve idea of romance."

Bronx grabbed Aurora Dawn's hand and dragged her across the room to the front door and outside onto the circular driveway.

Aurora Dawn lifted her dress off the pavement. "Bronx, my dress. You'll rip it."

"What's the difference, if you're not going to wear it for our wedding? We'll go see this Incredible Hulk and you can get him out of your system. You said yourself you can't marry him. You obviously care for me and we will work this out. Trust me. You can't leave our parents and all the guests hanging. You won't disappoint them. The honeymoon is already paid for. And I will have you. I've waited long enough."

"Let go, Bronx. You're hurting me."

"Well, then you know how it feels," he said, his voice breaking.

They got to the front door of the neighboring house, and Bronx pounded on the door.

"Lakeland, are you in there?"

The door swung open, and Bronx looked up at the giant who was standing there.

"You're Lancelot?"

Lance thrust out his hand. "I'm Lance Lakeland. You must be Bronx. I've heard a lot about you."

"That's funny. Because I haven't heard a damn thing about you until a few minutes ago. What are you trying to pull here?" Bronx glanced at his watch. "Aurora Dawn is going to be my wife in less than an hour."

Lance looked at Aurora Dawn with hungry eyes. "You look beautiful in your wedding dress. Come in."

Aurora Dawn smiled nervously. "We can only stay

a minute. Are your parents home?" she asked.

"They're still asleep. They're late risers."

Lance offered Aurora Dawn and Bronx a seat on the couch in the keeping room, but Bronx, flexing his muscles, refused it.

"We're not staying. We have a wedding to get to. I want to know what's going on. I've known Aurora Dawn my whole life. You move in a week ago, and suddenly you're in love? Do you know how twisted that sounds?"

Lance looked at Aurora Dawn with longing. "It's not how long you've known someone. I know it's sudden, but I've been looking for Aurora Dawn my whole life."

"That's a bunch of romantic rubbish." He turned to Aurora Dawn. "You don't know a thing about this man. He could be a serial killer."

"He could be," she agreed. "I don't really know you, do I, Lance?"

"You know all you need to know about me. You know my heart."

"Lakeland, we have a houseful of guests next door, waiting for a wedding. We can't just call it off at the last minute."

"I would gladly marry her right now."

"You don't get to hijack my wedding."

Lance rose to his full height and his presence filled the room. He looked like he was about to take flight. Bronx shrank back.

"I think that's Aurora Dawn's decision. I want to spend the rest of my life with her."

"So do I." He turned to his fiancée. "Aurora Dawn, please take some time to think about this."

Aurora Dawn sized up the two men in the room. Bronx was a known quantity. But he was going off the deep end. Lance was a wild card. She was drawn to him, but he wasn't who he had claimed to be. She knew what her life would be like with Bronx. Life with Lance would be an unknown. The chemistry with Lance was off the charts, but a person couldn't live on love or lust alone.

She thought of all of the people, her friends and family, waiting next door. All the money her parents had spent on the wedding. The embarrassment she would cause Bronx and his parents, her parents, if she left him at the altar. How long had she known Lance? Less than a week. Bronx was right. Lance was a virtual stranger.

"Bronx, take me home."

Lance turned pale. "Aurora Dawn, please, reconsider."

"I've made my decision. It's final."

Bronx slung his arm around Aurora Dawn's waist, tried to hold up her train, and walked her out the door, as far away from Lance and as fast as he could possibly go.

Chapter Nineteen

Out of breath, Bronx and Aurora Dawn clung to each other, panting in the foyer of her mansion.

"Are we good?" Bronx asked. "Do I have your word?"

Aurora Dawn nodded. She'd never broken a promise in her life. There was no going back.

The wedding planner rushed in. "There you are. You're not supposed to see the groom before the wedding. Your hair is a mess. Come upstairs and let me make repairs."

"Aurora Dawn? Promise?" Bronx took her hand and searched her face until she met his gaze.

"Yes."

"That's my girl." Bronx gave her a quick kiss on the cheek and strode away confidently with a bounce in his step.

"Is there a problem?" asked the wedding planner.

"There was," Aurora Dawn said softly, "but not anymore."

"Good. Your mother is upstairs waiting with your bridesmaids. We're almost ready for the processional." The wedding planner followed her up the circular staircase.

Aurora Dawn entered her bedroom, examined herself in the cheval mirror, and went to the window. Lance was there, looking back at her, his eyes entreating her. If she had her way, she'd let down her hair and call out to him. But she'd already made her decision. And her hair was no longer loose around her shoulders. It was done up in a French twist, the way Bronx liked it. She turned away. From her window. From Lance. And looked toward her future.

"Darling," Kate whispered, closing the balloon shades. "I have something for you."

Kate handed her a jewelry box.

"Open it."

Aurora Dawn untied the ribbon and opened the box.

"These are your best pearls."

"Your father gave them to me on our wedding day. I want you to have them."

"They're beautiful. Will you put them on me?"

"Of course." Kate lifted the pearls and placed them around her daughter's neck, affixing the diamond clasp. They looked good with her grandmother's amulet.

"You are going to be the most beautiful bride. Your father and I are so happy for you, and so proud."

Tears glistened in Kate's eyes.

"Mom, don't cry."

"It's not every day that your only daughter gets married." She hugged her daughter.

The wedding planner cleared her throat, making her presence known. "I think the bride needs a little more work. I'll have her ready to walk down the aisle in a minute."

The wedding planner straightened Aurora Dawn's tilted tiara and fixed her hair. Then she wiped the perspiration from Aurora Dawn's brow with her handkerchief. "I think you got a little overheated. It's warm outside. You're feeling a little anxious. That's to be expected. You'll be a bride in no time."

Time was running out. Lance's sorrow was so strong, she felt it from across the lawn, through the tangle of the brambles. He was losing his one true love. The enchanted forest was encroaching again.

"Lance, I love you," Aurora Dawn thought. "But I can't marry you. We're from two different worlds."

The wedding march sounded in the room below.

"Well, it's time," the wedding planner exclaimed, lining up the bridesmaids, groomsmen, parents of the couple, and the bride, all in marching order. "Is everybody ready? Go on my signal."

Aurora Dawn moved forward woodenly as she wrestled with her broken dreams and broken heart. She struggled to lift her feet, which seemed set in stone. Her head throbbed. She felt faint. She sent out a silent cry for help, a heartfelt message to her Lancelot. Short of his barging in on the wedding ceremony—à la Dustin Hoffman's *The Graduate* style—and stealing her away, it was the end of their story.

"Goodbye, my love," she whispered under her breath.

Chapter Twenty

The Wedding

"I've lost her." Lance sat slumped on the couch in the keeping room, dejection pasted on his face like a thick cucumber facial. Earlier, his true love had been resting in his arms, the possibility of a bright future looming. Then he had experienced a pang of conscience when he decided to be honest about his past, snatching all hope from the relationship. The expression, "No good deed goes unpunished," came to mind.

"I'm an idiot." Lance wanted to scream, so he did, causing Gwenn to come running up from the basement.

"What on earth is the matter? They can hear you all the way in the Underworld."

Lance tilted his head and looked askew at his "mother."

"It's over." Lance sighed. "We were so close, and then I told her about Gedeon."

"Lancelot Lakeland, sit up straight and listen to your mother."

Lance didn't move. He didn't have the stamina or the will to go on. He was stuck in the sludge of his past.

"Are you going to sit around feeling sorry for yourself? Or are you going to go next door and get the girl?"

Lance's eyelids drooped. "She's getting married,

right this minute, to that loser Bronx Bamberger. She hates me."

"She doesn't hate you. I saw the way that girl looked at you. She's just conflicted. That's a lot to take in, finding out that the man you're in love with is a vampire, and not a very nice one." Gwenn took a deep breath and continued. "Would Gedeon Nagy sit around and mope if he wanted a woman? No, he would fly over and take her."

"I can't fly," said Lance desolately.

"You can walk, can't you? Are you just going to accept defeat, or are you going to fight for the girl?"

"She doesn't want me. I've tried to change. But I can't escape my past."

"If she was truly in love with you, she wouldn't want you to change. She'd accept you as you are. A deliciously sexy specimen of—whatever you are."

"Thanks. But you didn't see the look of distaste on her face. She was horrified when she learned the truth."

"Would it do any good to tell you there are other fish in the sea? How about a delectable mermaid? I could hook you up with one your father and I met in a club in Midtown last night."

"You met a mermaid in Midtown?"

"Yes, they had a mini-aquarium and she was swimming in the tank, half naked. Your father almost tripped over himself trying to get a seat in front of the tank. The woman had magnificent breasts, the kind of breasts Gedeon would have loved."

Lance pouted. "I'm not Gedeon. And I don't want just any fish or any breasts. I want Aurora Dawn."

"That's boring and pathetic. You used to be a man of taste, and you took a bite out of any woman who came along. As I recall, you weren't very discriminating."

"That was then, and this is now. I know what I want."

"Then get off your mortal duff and go after it. Or you'll regret it for the rest of your life, however long that may be."

"How do you propose I do that? Crash the wedding and snatch the bride?"

"That's one way," said Gwenn. "Or you could be a little more dramatic. For instance, you could walk out the front door and mount your white steed, Excalibur, ride into the Crystal Palace, and rescue the maiden in distress."

Lance straightened. "There's a white steed in the driveway?"

"Your father and I dropped into a horse farm in Alpharetta and picked out a magnificent Arabian for the occasion. He's quite magical, actually."

Lance brightened and walked to the front door. He opened it.

"Excalibur?" The horse neighed his assent.

"It's a sign," said Gwenn.

"He's a champion. You stole him?"

"I prefer to use the term 'borrowed,' darling. You can still ride, can't you?"

"Of course."

Lancelot circled the horse and put his broad hands on the beast's mane, rubbing her gently. "She's a beauty."

"She loves being ridden. Your father tried her out. Put her through her paces. He said he's going to show me his own Excalibur later on in the bedroom."

Lancelot rolled his eyes. "Arthur is a sod."

Gwenn sighed. "I know, but he's my sod."

"I'm not dressed for a wedding," Lance objected. "Clothes make the man."

"Honey, you couldn't be more of a man if you rode in there naked. It doesn't matter what you wear. It's who you are. You're a good man. You're in love. Now go get the girl, Romeo."

"Thanks, Mom," Lance said, smiling. He leaped up, his heart flying, mounted Excalibur, and rode off into the sunset.

"I hope I'm not too late."

Chapter Twenty-One

Aurora Dawn descended the staircase, following the bridal party. When she rounded the corner, everyone in the ballroom stood and gasped.

"Breathtaking! Lovely. She's a princess. Look at that gown! It was made for her body." Aurora Dawn wanted to smile, but her heart was heavy.

"Lance, my love," she thought. "It's too late."

Her father tucked her elbow into his. "Aurora Dawn, sweetheart, you're shaking."

"Daddy…" Her voice quivered.

"What is it, Princess?"

"I can't," she whispered. "I don't… I want…"

Jack tightened his grip on his daughter. "What do you want?"

"I want Lance," she said, barely breathing.

"Shit," Jack said. At that moment Kate took her daughter's other arm, holding her up.

"Darling, what's wrong? You look positively pallid."

"She wants Lance," Jack whispered hoarsely. "What are we going to do?"

"We're going to continue walking down the aisle," Kate asserted. "This can't be happening. Aurora Dawn, this is just your nerves talking," she assured her daughter. "You're going to be okay. Everything is going to be okay. There's Bronx. He's waiting for you.

Only a few steps more. You can do it. We can do it together."

Aurora Dawn's hands shook. She began hyperventilating. "Daddy," she cried. "Help me! I can't do this."

"Kate, do something. Talk to your daughter."

"Aurora Dawn," her mother pleaded. "Don't cry. You'll ruin your makeup."

They were halfway down the rose-strewn aisle.

Aurora Dawn sniffled. She looked straight ahead as she addressed her mother. "Don't make me do this."

"It's out of our hands, now," Kate reasoned. "You're going to get married."

Aurora Dawn screamed silently.

Outside the door, Lance dismounted, opened the door, and remounted Excalibur.

He heard Aurora Dawn cry out.

"Aurora Dawn," he shouted, riding down the aisle toward the bridal procession.

"Lancelot," she answered. "Lance, I'm here."

"I'm coming, darling."

The horse cantered. The guests began to whisper loudly. Lance brought the animal directly behind Aurora Dawn, and a hoof came down on her gown, stopping her in her tracks. Lance dismounted.

He turned her around, and her parents broke away.

He got down on his knees. "Aurora Dawn Hale, I love you with all my heart. Come away with me."

Aurora Dawn jumped into his arms. "You came! You rode in on a white horse to rescue me. I knew you would come for me. Lance, I love you. Yes, I'll go with you."

Bronx reddened and started down the aisle.

"Aurora Dawn!" he shouted. "What are you doing?"

"Bronx, I'm sorry," she said apologetically. "I can't marry you."

Lightbulbs flashed. Guests whipped out their cell phones to document the disaster.

Lance didn't hesitate. He swept Aurora Dawn off her feet, gathered her veil and her train in his arms, placed her on Excalibur, and leapt up behind her. He backed Excalibur down the aisle and out into the foyer.

Juliette was blocking the door.

"Do you love this young man?" she demanded.

Aurora Dawn grasped the amethyst necklace her grandmother had given her for protection. She knew she couldn't pass without her grandmother's permission. Hers was a deep magic.

"With all my heart and soul," Aurora Dawn answered.

"Then go and be happy."

Juliette opened the door, and Lance and Aurora Dawn rode out to greet their future.

Chapter Twenty-Two

Aurora Dawn turned around on the horse, her head sinking into Lance's broad chest. Lance could feel her smile through his cotton shirt. He wore the same silly grin. They were free. They were together. No matter what came next.

Lance directed the steed down Aurora Dawn's driveway and back up into his driveway.

"That was a narrow escape," Lance said.

"I knew you'd come for me."

Lance dismounted and lifted his bride to the ground and kissed her.

"I'm sorry I ruined your wedding. You looked—you look beautiful, and I can't wait to marry you. And then I want to make love to you and never stop."

Aurora Dawn giggled. "I know where we can find someone to marry us."

Aurora Dawn borrowed Lance's cell phone and called her mother.

"Aurora Dawn, where are you, young lady?" She heard her mother whisper, "Jack, it's Aurora Dawn."

"Not far," she answered. "In fact, I'm right next door. Are you mad?"

"I don't know the word for what I'm feeling."

"Is Bronx still there?"

"No, Bronx and his parents ducked out right after you left. Then the entire groom's side made their exit.

Our side is still sitting there expectantly, wondering what happened. I doubt we'll be hearing from the Bambergers anytime soon if ever again. Betsey is devastated."

"I have a proposition for you."

"I'm listening."

'Are there any officiants left?'

"The rabbi left with the Bambergers to help calm Betsey down, but Reverend Hunter is still here. He's trying to explain to the guests what defies explanation. This is going to be all over the papers and the Internet."

"We should be used to that by now," Aurora Dawn said. "Mom, Lance and I want to get married, right away. I'm already in my wedding dress. Can you keep the guests there, and Lance and I will come back over?"

"You don't have a marriage license. Well, not the right one, anyway."

"Is the governor still there? Can we get him to intervene?"

Kate sighed. "I can ask him."

"And after the religious ceremony, we can go downtown to the courthouse and fill out the necessary paperwork to get our license."

"Let me alert the guests. How long will you be?"

"As long as it takes Lance to find a suit."

"I have a tux," Lance reported. "I'll get dressed and tell my parents to get ready."

"Aurora Dawn, are you sure about this? You barely know this boy. And what you do know is troubling. There are so many unanswered questions. Are you sure you're not rushing into this marriage?"

Aurora Dawn reached for Lance's hand. "I have never been so sure of anything in my life."

"Then I'll see you soon."

"Are you happy?" Lance asked his bride-to-be.

"Happier than I've ever been," she assured him.

****

Gwenn put the finishing touches on her makeup while Art straightened Lance's tie.

"Where will you live?"

"I thought we'd stay here in the mansion."

"What about a honeymoon?"

"I would fly my bride around the world if I could, but we'll have to fly commercial."

"Then I guess our work here is done."

"I appreciate everything you've done for me. If it hadn't been for you, Aurora Dawn would have been married to Bronx Bamberger by now."

"We only gave you a push. You went after what you wanted. I hope you'll be very happy."

"Where will you go?"

"I'm sure the count will have another assignment for us."

"Thanks, 'Mom,' " Lance said, hugging her.

"The count told me to tell you you'll be well taken care of."

Lance looked puzzled.

"He's opened a bank account in your name. All the documents you need are in the study."

"That was very generous of him."

"He knows he owes you, after the way he left you. Your mortality is a big question mark."

"None of that matters now that I have Aurora Dawn."

Chapter Twenty-Three

Lance carried his bride over the threshold of the Stryer mansion.

"You're home, Mrs. Lakeland."

"Is that really your name?"

Lance smiled sheepishly. "No."

"Are Gwenn and Art really your parents?"

Lance shook his head. "No."

"Good. They were a bit over the top. Will they be living with us?"

"No, they're no longer here. This is our home."

"If we live here, I'll have to redecorate, and definitely repaint the outside," Aurora Dawn said when Lance deposited her on the hideous couch in the keeping room.

"We have plenty of room, room for a family of our own. In fact, I'd like to get started on that project right away."

Aurora Dawn blushed. "But first, should I call you Lance or Gedeon?"

"When I look at you, I want to be good. Gedeon was not good."

"When I look at you, I see a clean soul. I want to know you, every part of you, the good and the bad. No secrets between us ever again."

Lance kissed her lips and began removing her wedding gown.

"Shouldn't we start in the bedroom?"

"I can't wait," Lance growled, unhooking her bra as Aurora Dawn wriggled out of her panties. She shivered. "Are you cold?"

"No, my love, but maybe just a little scared."

"I don't bite," Lance said, pausing to kiss her nipples gently. "I mean, not anymore."

"Do you want to bite me?" Aurora Dawn teased.

Lance finished undressing and flexed his wrist as he began to massage her and gnaw on her neck.

"What does that feel like?"

"Honestly, when I feel your blood flow against my lips, I want to… It's hard to break a centuries-old habit."

Aurora Dawn's body tingled wherever he touched. His hand on her body was like a brand.

"I want to feel you. Take me, and don't hold back." She bit his lip until it bled.

"You've drawn blood, you little temptress." Lance looked at her. "You've restored me. I want to give you the world, fly you to Paris, but the world is no longer mine to give."

"Then give me your body and your soul now and forever, my love."

In her arms, he could fly. Lance raised himself over her, unleashed his power, and gentled her with drugging kisses. He didn't need to glamour her. She was already under his spell, bucking naked, restless, hot and wet beneath him like an enchantress. His tongue and mouth worked its magic in all her secret places until she was begging him for release.

He lowered himself into her and knew he was home. As he moved inside her, she met him, matching his rhythm until they were lost in each other.

"My sweet pet, my little one, my beloved," he said, whispering endearments in a language she couldn't understand.

"Lance," she cried out. "I love you."

She had called him Lance. She could give him no better gift. She loved him, flaws and all. She loved and accepted him for the man he was now. There were no more thoughts of Marika, only of the woman in his arms. He cried out her name in ecstasy. Finally, he slept, peaceful dreams, no thoughts of demons or dungeons, only peace, sweet peace, at last.

Chapter Twenty-Four

"I can't believe the wedding is over," said Jack, relaxing on the couch in the living room with his wife. Wedding gifts were stacked almost to the ceiling.

"I can't believe our daughter is married to a vampire."

"Kate, there are no such things as vampires."

"Then how do you explain what happened in Bermuda and the Nagy Chronicles?"

"Lance's distant relative. The boy is in his twenties."

"What are we going to do?"

"I've offered him a job with the agency, and he's accepted."

"Why would you do that?"

"Haven't you heard the expression, 'Keep your friends close and your enemies closer?' "

"He's not our enemy. He's our son-in-law."

"If we alienate Aurora Dawn, we'll lose her forever. And I could use the help, with Will retiring."

"My mother believes in vampires, but she's accepted Lance—or Gedeon, or whatever his name is—into the family."

"The Bambergers will never forgive us."

"Aurora Dawn was not in love with Bronx. It would have been a disastrous marriage."

"You are probably right. And I've never seen

Aurora Dawn so happy. She came back from the honeymoon starry-eyed."

"And probably pregnant."

"We got pregnant on our honeymoon, if I recall."

"I recall it very well." Jack wrapped his arms around his wife and kissed her.

"What kind of children do you think they'll have? Little vampires?"

"I thought we didn't believe in vampires."

"I don't know what to believe, Jack."

"Have some faith. It's obvious the kids are in love."

Kate sighed. "When does Lance start?"

"As soon as they get settled. I've already got cases stacked up that I couldn't get to until after the wedding."

Chapter Twenty-Five

Jack sat down in his office chair facing his new son-in-law. In his career, he'd faced down serial killers and drug dealers, drive-by shooters and gang leaders. But how did you communicate with a vampire? More specifically, a vampire who was married to your daughter. There was no rule book for a situation that defied the rules.

"So what shall I call you, Gedeon or Lance?"

"I'd prefer Lance. Gedeon is out of the picture."

"Level with me. Are you really a vampire, out to steal my daughter's soul?"

"As hard as this is to believe, I was a vampire, but now I'm simply a mortal man."

"Son, there's nothing simple about this. I don't know what to believe. But I do know that my daughter loves you, which means we have to work together. Are you prepared to do that?"

"Yes," Lance answered honestly.

"Well, then, let's get started." Jack dropped a case file in front of Lance.

Chapter Twenty-Six

"Honey, I'm home."

Aurora Dawn ran out from the kitchen and into Lance's arms.

"How was your day?"

"Those words are music to my ears," Lance admitted. "Considering the way I used to spend my days, hidden away, dodging the sun. Anyway, my day was pretty good. Your father and I reviewed some pending cases. I think I brought a fresh perspective to the table. He still doesn't know what to make of me. But all in all, I think things went pretty well."

Aurora Dawn wrapped her arms around Lance's neck and kissed him.

"That was worth coming home to."

"I'm so proud of you." Aurora Dawn hesitated. "Do you miss it?"

"Miss what?"

"Trolling for victims."

"Very funny. That's not all I did."

"But you like being on the right side of the law?"

"I like it a lot. But I love being home with you more." Lance picked up his wife, twirled her around, and planted kisses on her lips that left her breathless.

"Lance, dinner is almost on the table. That can wait."

"No, it can't. I've gone my whole life without

food, but I can't survive without your kisses." Lance reached under Aurora Dawn's tight knit sweater. His tongue danced with hers. "Why don't we take this conversation upstairs to our bedroom?"

"Lance, the dinner will burn."

"I'm the one who's burning."

Lance's hands explored his wife's body, her breasts, her stomach, and then his hands skimmed lower.

"Lance," Aurora Dawn said, "Please."

"Please what?"

"What about dinner?"

"Why don't you turn off the oven? Dinner can wait. I can't."

Aurora Dawn untangled herself from her husband and went into the kitchen to put dinner on hold. When she came out, she was wearing nothing but an apron.

"Now that's what I call a homecoming," Lance said. He lifted his wife off her feet and carried her upstairs like she was as light as a feather.

"Lance, are you getting stronger?"

"You noticed?"

"Yes, what's happening to you?"

"I don't know. I am experiencing some changes."

He deposited Aurora Dawn on the bed. "Give me some vampire love."

They rolled around on the bed as she tugged off his clothes. He removed her apron.

"I think you're getting friskier," she said playfully.

"Well, we're still on our honeymoon. Suddenly I'm getting hungry. Hungry for you, my little hors d'oeuvre."

"Oh, Lance," Aurora Dawn sighed. "You're

insatiable."

"Are you complaining?" he asked, straddling her.

"No," she said. "Not a bit."

When their pre-dinner interlude was over, Lance drifted into a deep sleep. Aurora Dawn decided not to wake him, and she tiptoed downstairs.

****

"Marika," Lance called out hoarsely, still groggy from sleep.

"Now, that's a name I haven't heard in a while."

"Zoltan, what are you doing here? Am I dreaming?"

"I put you in a dream state so we could talk. Have you noticed the changes?"

Lance frowned.

"In your body." Zoltan rubbed his tongue on his lower lip, touched a lock of Lance's hair and caressed his shoulder. "I've missed you."

Lance sat up, naked, and pushed his Maker's hand away.

"You have noticed. I've been watching you. There is a way to get it all back. Your power, your immortality. We could start over."

Lance glared at Zoltan. "I'm married, Zoltan, and happy. Happier than I've ever been. You're not making any sense. I thought, after the boat that morning, I was no longer what I once was."

"Apparently I was wrong," Zoltan whispered. "Gedeon, you have the most magnificent body. I've thought of little else since we parted."

"What are you saying?"

"Your body is with Aurora Dawn, but your mind is still on Marika. Have you tried to fly? You're still a fledgling, but you're growing stronger every day. What I'm saying is that you could be what you once were. If I were to…"

Zoltan inhaled and rubbed Lance's neck, breathing erratically. He lowered his mouth and wet Lance's skin with his tongue. His eyes rolled back in his head. "If I were to leave my mark on you, you would become immortal again. Think of it. You would have multiple lifetimes to enjoy. We could have multiple lifetimes together."

"I'm satisfied with this one lifetime, with Aurora Dawn."

"You could still have your little pet princess…and eat her too. And any other woman you wanted."

"She's the only woman I want."

"Imagine what it will be like to grow old and watch Aurora Dawn grow old."

"We would grow old together."

"You could turn her, if you cared to."

"And condemn her to the life I led? I would never do that to her."

"Come now. I've tapped into your dreams. I feel your need. You are dying to take a bite of her."

"I tamp down on those urges."

"Why deny yourself?"

Zoltan rubbed Lance's neck. "One simple bite, my love, and you could have it all back."

Repulsed, Lance pulled away from his Maker and rose from the bed.

"You were a god," Zoltan said, choking up. "You could be again. Do you remember what it was like between us?"

"I'm not that creature anymore. I'm not your

creature. I'm a human. A man who loves his wife. I have no desire to go back to you, to Marika, or to the way I was. You put her in my brain. I have not thought of Marika since I've been with Aurora Dawn."

"If it's the girl you want, you could make her yours forever."

"I would never tie her to me against her will," Lance insisted. "She is with me because she loves me."

"Love is highly overrated. But if you're worried, we could include her. She is a tempting bit of flesh. I wouldn't turn her out of our bed. I could glamour her, and she would beg for it. As I recall, you used to favor our little threesomes." Zoltan looked longingly at Lance and rubbed the pad of his thumb slowly across his bottom lip.

Lance fidgeted under his Maker's scrutiny and became increasingly uncomfortable. "I think you'd better go. You've made your offer, and you have my answer. I'd rather you not return."

Zoltan rose to his full height. "You think you can swat me away like an annoying fly? There will come a time when you will want me, want what we shared together."

"That will never happen. That never should have happened."

"I made you who you are," Zoltan said, enraged. "You owe me everything."

"You took my life, the life I could have had. Now I have another chance at happiness. I will never give that up. Stay away from me and my wife."

"You're playing with fire," Zoltan warned, rubbing Lance's single singed brow with the thumb of his other hand. "And you know what happens to bad boys who play with fire."

Zoltan wrapped himself in his long black cape and disappeared with a hiss.

At that moment, Aurora Dawn appeared in the bedroom, unaware of the events that had just taken place. She felt his forehead. "Darling, you're burning up. Do you have a fever?"

Lance shook his head. "Just a nightmare. I need a bath to wipe away the filth."

Aurora Dawn looked puzzled, but Lance grabbed her and held on for dear life to chase away her fears and calm his nerves. Zoltan Nagy was not through with them. He would be back, and when he came, Lance would be ready. As he grew stronger, he would regain the power to banish Zoltan from their lives forever.

Chapter Twenty-Seven

Lance tried out his office chair as his father-in-law entered the room.

"How do you like your new office?" Jack asked. "Or, I should say, Will Bradley's old office."

"Aurora Dawn's grandfather has already been here three times asking if I need anything."

Jack laughed. "That man doesn't know the meaning of retirement. What he needs to do is take his wife on a long vacation. He certainly deserves it. And she does too. If he's hovering too much, let me know."

Jack grabbed a chair, turned it around, and straddled it.

"Have you given any more thought to the case file I gave you yesterday?"

"That's all I've thought about, and I have some ideas I'd like to run by you."

"Let's hear them."

"It seems we have on our hands a brand-new type of serial killer. One who can enter houses undetected. Alarms present no challenge. I'm afraid I may know who is behind these crimes."

"What are you afraid of?"

"Mr. Hale, I'm afraid you won't believe me, but I think the people you're looking for are my people, or *were* my people. Your killers are vampires."

Jack hesitated. "That's unbelievable. But let's say I

do believe you. How would you bring those…people… to justice?"

"There are ways."

"Why would these people be interested in killing young boys?"

Lance thought back to his centuries as a vampire. "Because they can. Why does anyone kill—human or vampire? For the blood lust, yes, but then it often becomes a feeding frenzy, especially when more than one of them attack, and often the young, well, they don't survive the experience."

"Are there many of you, of them, in the world?"

Lance laughed. For a man who plied his trade in evil, his father-in-law was very naïve. He had no idea what he was up against, the vast army of vampires, masquerading as ordinary people in the world. Mayors and governors, yes, even senators, law enforcement officers, dictators—many of those, and soldiers. Anyone who had a blood lust or blood fever. Who craved human flesh. He had been one of their legions. He hadn't given a thought to taking a life for his pleasure or for sport.

He was so glad to be free of them. To walk out into the light, to enjoy regular food, and to have someone to love like Aurora Dawn. He would never go back to that depraved existence.

"We have, they have, been killing for centuries. You don't believe in their existence, so they are virtually untouchable. We can't wipe them out, but if the vampires you're looking for encroach on human territory, then they are fair game, if they can be caught."

"And you think the monsters kidnapping the young

boys are vampires?"

"I know the pattern, and yes, I think that's who you are looking for."

"What do you propose we do about it?"

"I have a plan. I will go undercover as a vampire, find out who's responsible, and bring them in."

Jack scratched his head. "That would be very dangerous. You're married to my daughter now. I can't let you take that risk."

"Without me, you'll never find them. If I can't capture them, we can at least discourage them from trolling in our city."

"It's a brilliant plan, but how will you protect my daughter if you start fraternizing with them again? They could try to exact revenge against your family."

"I would die before I'd ever let any one of them near Aurora Dawn."

It was tough talk. Inside Lance was shaking in fear for his wife.

Chapter Twenty-Eight

"My dear." The voice in her head, oily smooth, could charm a snake. Aurora Dawn rubbed her eyes and sat up in bed. Her evil-detecting spidey sense kicked into high gear.

When she saw his face, she startled and covered herself with the bedsheet. She had gone to sleep in a sheer negligee, but that had soon come off and stayed off. Her new husband didn't need a sexy nightgown to become aroused.

"Who are you, and what are you doing in my bedroom?"

"Relax," flowed the voice, as smooth as caramel, like the voice of the Devil, sucking out the light and air from the room and lulling her into complacency. "I'm Zoltan, a good friend of your husband's."

Zoltan. The count in the chronicles. The being who had turned Gedeon. Not good. She lifted her head proudly. She would not let him smell her fear.

"My husband isn't home."

"I didn't come to see your husband."

"How did you get in here?"

Zoltan laughed. "I go where I please."

"Then would you please wait downstairs while I get dressed? I'll meet you in the keeping room. It's—"

"I know my way around your house," Zoltan said.

When had he ever been in this house? She would

have to ask Lance about it.

Zoltan smirked, and his eyes followed her intently, signaling that he would rather stay and watch her get dressed. His gaze fixed on her breasts, which were burning underneath the sheets. The being probably had x-ray vision.

"If I must," he said finally, wrapping himself in his cape and disappearing.

'I was going to say, 'Use the stairs.' " Apparently, vampires had other means of transportation than walking like mere mortals.

"Lance?" she called, hoping that Lance hadn't left yet for work at her parents' psychic detective agency in their offices in the Crystal Palace compound next door. Lance was determined to make a good impression, and he had big ideas he wanted to present to her father.

Aurora Dawn dressed and walked downstairs. She would just see what the count wanted and send him on his way. She wrapped her hand around her grandmother's protective amulet. No harm could come to her while she was wearing it. It couldn't be removed forcibly. She would have to give it up. And that she would never do.

"Count Nagy," she said, walking into the keeping room.

The count gazed at her. She was dressed in a yellow T-shirt dress, reflecting all the goodness and light within her and all the delicious curves of her delectable body. "Gedeon described you to me, but he didn't do you justice. You're even more lovely in person."

Had he seen her picture? Looked into her mind as she could into his? He was certainly doing that now.

She was powerless to block him. She clasped her arms to her shoulders.

"You don't have to be afraid of me. I've simply come to offer you a wedding gift."

Aurora Dawn was wary. "I'm not afraid of you. I don't need a wedding gift."

"It's a gift you could give your husband."

"What gift would that be?"

"Eternal life."

Aurora Dawn smoothed her hand over her forehead to try to block him. "I don't understand."

"You know Gedeon chose to live a mortal life with you. But he already regrets that."

"He told you that?"

"We spoke, and I offered him immortality. He would take it were it not for you. He doesn't want to live without you. But if you would join him in that exalted state, you could be together forever."

"H-how would that happen?"

Zoltan laughed. "In the regular way, the regular way of the vampire."

He reached out and skimmed Aurora Dawn's neck with his knuckles. She sprang back, repelling the untoward, unwanted contact.

"Oh, it's nothing sexual," he purred, running his tongue along his bottom lip. "It won't hurt a bit."

Aurora Dawn was surprised. How many times had Lance told her he had everything he wanted or needed in their marriage? But maybe he'd wanted to spare her feelings. If it was in her power to grant him what he wished for, how could she hold back? She would give up everything she had to make him happy.

"I will ask him what he thinks," Aurora Dawn said.

"I have no secrets from my husband."

"No secrets? You are very naïve, my dear. Has he told you about Marika?"

Aurora Dawn chewed on her bottom lip. "I know who she is…was."

Zoltan tilted his head. "It would be good to have a secret of your own. I wouldn't tell your husband about this. Let it be a surprise."

Aurora Dawn wavered, rubbing her neck gingerly as if she had been scalded. Her whole life would change. But she and Lance could be, would be, united forever.

"Tell me exactly how it would work," she pressed.

Zoltan smiled. He knew he had her.

"Would it happen here? Would Lance be with me?"

"It could happen here," Zoltan explained. "And of course we could perform the ceremony together, the three of us. But wouldn't it be so much better if we went back to the source, where Gedeon was first turned, back to Hungary?"

"We? Would I be tied to you?"

"My dear, you've been reading too much vampire lore. I would be your Maker and Gedeon's Maker, but you would be free spirits to live your lives as you please, where you please. Let me give you a little demonstration. Step closer."

Aurora Dawn hesitated.

"I won't bite." Zoltan threw his head back and howled with laughter. "A little vampire humor."

He took Aurora Dawn's arm and brought her in toward his body. He caressed her neck, then lightly kissed it, lingering on the spot with his tongue.

"My mark would go here."

Aurora Dawn shivered.

"It won't burn. I will glamour you so you won't feel a thing. It will be over quickly."

She took shallow breaths and tried to pull away, but she couldn't control her body. She could read his thoughts and knew the things he wanted to do with her, to her, beyond the bite. She saw an image of them spinning naked up to the sky in a dark funnel cloud. He would transport her to his world, to new heights, he was thinking. He wanted to possess her, but more than that, he wanted to possess Lance. Was it worth the sacrifice?

"Please stop," she pleaded. "Go now. I will belong to no one but my husband."

"Of course, I can turn Gedeon, and he can turn you. As I said, the experience need not be sexual, but it can be, and when it is, it will take you to new heights of awareness *and pleasure*. There would be no earthly limits."

Zoltan strummed her neck gently with the back of his fingers, weaving his spell. He was hypnotizing her.

"My darling, Eve, you have to take but one bite of the apple, and you'll be in paradise."

Aurora Dawn felt Zoltan's hot breath on her neck. "I don't know."

"You are doing the right thing. Trust me."

Chapter Twenty-Nine

Aurora Dawn lit scented candles in the bedroom and dressed in a gauzy nightgown of gray mist. She sprayed perfume along her neck and between her breasts. It was a concoction her grandmother had created and named after her granddaughter. Lance would not be able to resist her. She made the moment magic with music, "The Burning Ring of Fire," their song. And when he came home, after they made love, she would announce her surprise. A sacrifice he would never ask her to make, but one she would make for him. He would be so happy. She couldn't wait to see the expression on his face.

She heard Lance downstairs and called out to him, "I'm up here, darling."

Lance appeared in the bedroom doorway and looked at the scene Aurora Dawn had set.

"What is all this? It looks like a seduction."

"That's part of it," she said. "I have something to tell you."

"And I have something to tell you. I have to go undercover for a while, on assignment for your father."

Aurora Dawn was used to her parents working long and strange hours and often on undercover assignments.

"That's wonderful. But will it be dangerous?"

Lance hesitated. "It could be, but it's nothing I can't handle."

"Can you talk about the case?"

"Not really. But I'll have to be gone for several days, possibly a week. Now what did you want to tell me?"

Aurora Dawn smiled. "It's a surprise, but it can wait."

"But I can't." Lance took his bride into his arms and touched his lips to hers, which ignited the flame of desire that only she could quench. Lance gave as much pleasure as he got. *No earthly limits*, she thought, Zoltan's promise lingering in her mind.

Chapter Thirty

Lance took an overnight flight to Budapest. He flew coach, so his legs hardly fit under the seat in front of him. The flight was a long, uncomfortable eleven hours and thirty minutes. He rarely took commercial, but he couldn't exactly get to Zoltan's palace any other way. He mapped out his route. He'd rent a car, like any other ordinary man, and drive hours into the mountains, into the mist, to his Maker's home. This palace had been Zoltan's new residence ever since Zoltan deserted him to marry and start a dynasty. Gedeon's castle had been repossessed by the Hungarian government, and all his artwork removed. Not *his* artwork. Artwork stolen during World War II, now restored to its rightful owners.

He had mixed emotions about this assignment. Zoltan had been part of his life for centuries. He owed his allegiance to his Maker, but the count had also robbed him of his humanity and led him on the dark path. He hadn't wanted to see Zoltan again but he needed information only Zoltan could provide. Zoltan could be unpredictable. He only hoped he would survive the encounter.

****

"Gedeon," Zoltan said, hardly disguising the excitement in his voice when Lance was led into his library. "Warm your hands in front of the fire. Have you come home?"

"No," Lance answered honestly.

"Ah, you need something from me, then," Zoltan intuited, greeting his protégé warmly. "You know I could never deny you anything."

"I need information."

"How can I help you?"

Lance got right to the point.

"There have been a rash of kidnappings in Atlanta. Young boys lifted out of their beds, gone missing, never to be seen again. I'm working with Aurora Dawn's father to help solve the crimes."

Zoltan laughed.

"You find that funny?"

"There was a time when you would have seen the humor in the situation."

"It started in Aurora Dawn's neighborhood. I know Gwenn and Art were responsible for the first two kidnappings, but I made them return the boys before they did any lasting damage. Now it's starting again. It could be a copycat situation. But that's doubtful. The intruders are getting in through locked windows with the alarms set. Do you know who's responsible?"

Zoltan wound his arms behind his back and clasped his hands. "I may know. It would be so much easier if you were still one of us."

"I told you I would never return to that life."

"Never say never. What will you give me in return?"

Lance opened his palms toward the ceiling. "I have nothing to offer you."

Zoltan looked Lance up and down, his eyes lingering on Lance's angelic face, his thick lips, his muscular physique. "I could think of something."

"Our time together is over, Zoltan." Lance's tone was absolute.

Zoltan could barely hide his disappointment. "I suppose a little information couldn't hurt. I would be violating a trust, but those men mean nothing to me. As far as I'm concerned, they're dispensable."

Lance folded his arms and tapped his shoe impatiently.

"The illustrious Atlanta Police Department has been infiltrated by two of our brethren. The Harlan twins. You remember them, Tobias and Sebastian. As I recall, you were on hand for their initiation ceremony."

Lance remembered the brothers, but not fondly. They were loutish and brutal. He had been glad when they decided to leave the continent. Apparently, they had landed in Atlanta and never left.

"They're having quite a field day in your metropolis. It's open season for them. They get to carry weapons and assault citizens, and it's all quite legal for the men in blue."

"Are you sure about them?"

Zoltan nodded. "They're bragging about their exploits all over the network."

"Can they be stopped?" Lance inquired.

"There's only one way to stop a vampire, as you well know. Do you want to put them through the agony you experienced?"

"Kidnapping and killing children cannot be tolerated."

"Tsk, tsk. There's nothing more irritating than a reformed vampire."

"I know right from wrong," Lance stated.

"So do I," Zoltan retorted. "I just choose not to make that distinction. I'm not giving you carte blanche to destroy our American network. But if you want to put down those two rabid dogs, go right ahead, if you have the stomach for it."

Lance would have to consult with Aurora Dawn's father, who used to be a member of the APD. Perhaps they'd have to get Juliette, Aurora Dawn's grandmother, involved. They'd need all the reinforcements they could get.

"So now that I gave you what you need, there is something I need from you."

"I've already told you that is not in the stars."

"I have a feeling you will come back to me."

"Why would I do that?"

"Have you talked to your wife lately?"

"What does Aurora Dawn have to do with this?"

"Did she tell you I paid her a visit?"

"You came to my house?"

"It was my house first."

Lance wanted to rip Zoltan apart, but he was here on a fact-finding mission. He would have to tread lightly. He was not in a position of power. He decided to change the subject and put Zoltan on the defensive until he could get his temper under control. "I've been meaning to ask you. Do you know anything about the Stryer family that was murdered in that mansion next to the Crystal estate?"

The count got a faraway look in his eyes. He rubbed his chin, exhaled, and smiled.

"I remember that night like it was yesterday. I can still hear her screams when she begged for mercy and for the lives of her children. I can still smell the blood."

He sniffed the air as if he were recalling the dream of an alluring fragrance.

Lance tried to hide his distaste. "Why that family?"

"I was in Atlanta on business, and I saw the woman at a club. I wanted to party, and she didn't. She said she was married, but then why was she at the club alone, looking good enough to eat? She said she was with friends, but she wasn't. I followed her home. I waited until the middle of the night, and then I came into her bedroom. Her husband woke up and tried to stop me, so I had to kill him. But then we partied."

"She agreed to be with you after you slaughtered her husband in front of her?"

"Oh, she fought me at first, but when I threatened to wake her children, she stopped struggling. Her body was magnificent, and I feasted on it. I offered her a chance to be with me, for eternal life, but she wouldn't leave her children, so I had no choice but to drain them. They were very succulent and tender, but too weak to survive my supernatural strength."

"So what happened to the woman?"

"She went mad when I started playing with the children. The viperess tried to kill me, but of course, she couldn't get me off them once I had sunk my teeth into—well, you know how it is after a fresh kill. And then when I had my fill of the children, I tied her down on the bed, and we spent the night together, she and I. It was glorious. But I played too hard. I didn't mean to hurt her. But again, sometimes I don't know my own strength. A pity. But you know how that is."

Lance frowned. He had done that and worse.

"They never did solve that case. It was a bloodbath. The police had to keep the details out of the media.

They'd never seen anything like it."

"No, and they never will. There is no record of me in their DNA database. The house went up for sale, and when no one bought it, eventually I did, and I gifted the house to you and your beautiful bride."

Lance thought he was going to be sick at the thought of what had gone on in their bedroom all those years ago.

"You said you came to my house after the wedding?"

"Yes, and I met your beautiful bride. Woke her up, in fact. She sleeps in the nude, but I think you already know that."

Lance raised his hand to his Maker, but Zoltan caught it before Lance could throw a punch.

"Don't worry, I excused myself, and she got dressed and met me downstairs. She was cordial, but cool."

"If you hurt her, I'll kill you."

"Ah, so the truth finally comes out. Your idle threats don't scare me. I simply offered her a proposition."

"What do you mean?"

"I told her how much you missed your powers and how it was your greatest wish to be restored to your former self, but that you would never leave her. So I explained how much sense it would make if she were immortal, and you could be together forever."

"You had no right to interfere in my life or proposition my wife. I am very happy with my current situation, and she knows it."

Zoltan ran his thumb over Lance's singed brow. Lance recoiled.

"There was a time, my friend, when you found my touch to your liking."

"Our time has passed."

"Your bride would do anything to make you happy. I simply explained how she could make your fondest wish come true. Painted a picture of two lovers united in eternal bliss."

"Did you touch her?"

"She wondered how it might work, whether it would hurt." Zoltan flashed a Cheshire cat grin. "I told her there would be nothing sexual about the experience."

"I need to know. Did you follow through?"

"You'll have to ask your wife about that. She wants it to be a surprise." Zoltan reached out and stroked Lance's neck. "But then, perhaps you'd like me to put my mark on you now, so you can join her for all eternity."

Lance spun around and cast off Zoltan's advances. He spat in his Maker's face. "If you touched my wife, I will kill you. And you won't see me coming."

Lance had a sudden need to see his wife. Was she already marked? Had she submitted to Zoltan? Zoltan was hard to resist, and he almost always got what he wanted. He wanted Lance back, and he was not above using anyone or anything to achieve his goal.

When he returned to Atlanta, Lance would waste no time contacting Jack Hale. He'd provide the names of the two rogue cops in the department who were responsible for the recent rash of kidnappings. If they could track down the twins' residence, perhaps they might find the missing boys alive. He hoped it was not too late. They would need to develop a plan. But first he had to see Aurora Dawn and make sure she was unharmed. If Zoltan had already turned her, he would have no choice but to go back to the way he was. It filled him with a sense of dread to imagine his beautiful bride stripped of all her light and sweetness, doomed to live in darkness for eternity. He would kill Zoltan in the most painful way.

Chapter Thirty-One

Lance pulled into the garage of the Stryer mansion and searched the house for Aurora Dawn. He called her name several times, his heart racing, until he finally found her in the library, at the computer with headphones on, probably listening to Johnny Cash and writing her vampire stories. She was whole and safe. He stood there drinking in her beauty and walked up behind her and kissed her neck. She startled and turned around.

"Lance, you're home!" She jumped up into his arms and showered him with kisses.

He held her against his body as if she were weightless. His strength was returning more every day, and perhaps some of his powers.

"I missed you," Aurora Dawn whispered, "so much."

"I can see that."

"Did you have a good trip?"

"I got what I went for, but more than I bargained for."

"What do you mean?"

Lance put her down. "Let's go into the keeping room and talk."

Aurora Dawn removed her headphones, and they walked hand in hand into the keeping room. She sat next to him on the couch in front of the fireplace.

He lifted her hands. "Your hands feel warm. Are you feeling okay?" He could feel her blood flow and was grateful her skin wasn't cool to the touch.

"Of course, why wouldn't I be?"

Next, he bent her neck to his face. No marks. He would have recognized Zoltan's handiwork. He exhaled.

"I saw Zoltan."

Aurora Dawn frowned. Her hands began to shake.

"He told me you h-had a s-surprise for me." Lance wore a pained expression but hoped for the best. "He didn't, you know—"

"Turn me?" she whispered.

Lance held his breath.

"My love, he tried. He told me I would be fulfilling your fondest wish, and I would do anything to make your dreams come true."

"Not that!" Lance cried. "Never that. I am happy with my life, with you. I wouldn't change a thing. I wouldn't go back."

"I know that. I read him and could see his dishonorable intentions and the lengths he would go to have you. He wanted to turn me so that you would have no choice but to come to him, humble yourself before him, and beg him to take you back. But then he would own both of our souls. And you must know I would never submit to being used that way. That is a personal bond, and I would only agree to be bound to my husband. Lance, I wouldn't deny you anything. If you wanted to take me that way, I would agree and welcome you with an open heart. You have only to ask."

She offered her neck to Lance, and he caressed and

kissed it. He tamped down the urge to bite into her pristine white flesh. It was an urge so powerful it bordered on the sexual. But he bit it back before it overpowered both of them.

"I would never ask that of you. I would never damn you to the life I knew. I would rather live a short time with you on this earth than make you suffer an eternity with me."

"I knew that. And Lance, there is another reason. And that is my surprise."

He watched his wife expectantly.

She clasped her hands over her stomach. "Darling, we're going to have a baby."

Lance's mouth opened, his jaw hung slack and he raised his single brow.

"A baby?"

"Yes, isn't it wonderful?"

A blast of unrestrained joy shot through his heart. He could hardly stand the happiness. He didn't think it possible. He would be grateful for all eternity, for the eternity he had left on this earth. So this was what it felt like to be complete. He and Aurora Dawn had created a pure, pristine soul. But what if—

"Aren't you afraid of what my seed could produce? What if our child is a monster like me?"

Aurora Dawn placed her palm on his cheek. "Lance, my love, when I look into your eyes and into your heart and into your soul, I see a good man. I am proud to be your wife, and I know you will be a good father to our child." To our daughter, thought Aurora Dawn, for she knew with certainty that they had created a daughter to pass on the family's psychic heritage. But she would wait and let Lance find that out the normal way.

He pulled her toward him in a strong embrace.

"You're happy?"

"Beyond words. And that is why I turned down the count. I was afraid for our child. What would become of her...or him? I will take my chances with you and only you. I know you will protect us."

"With my life," he promised.

Chapter Thirty-Two

"Was your trip productive?" Jack asked.

"I think so," said Lance.

"What have you learned?"

"There are two brothers, Tobias and Sebastian Harlan. And they're in the Atlanta Police Department."

"I know the twins. They work the night shift in my old precinct. They give cops a bad name."

"They're sociopaths, both of them. And they're—"

"They're what?"

"They're also vampires."

Jack laughed. "Then it's true? We actually have vampires working in the APD?"

"I'm afraid it's much worse than that, sir. There are vampires all over this city and in almost every city in America. They have to live somewhere."

Jack pursed his lips. "I'm still having trouble wrapping my head around the fact that you are actually a vampire—or were a vampire—and that you're married to my daughter."

"They walk among us. The average person would have no idea until they cross a vampire's path, and then it's too late."

"Can you tell?"

"Of course. Some of your most well-known politicians, actors, and sports stars are vampires. That's why they seem superhuman—because they are."

"I can believe that. But when they're representing justice in the police department, I can't accept that. Are you positive?"

"I've seen them in action. They're merciless killers."

"So you think they're responsible for the kidnappings?"

"That's their style. And I have confirmation."

Jack rubbed his chin thoughtfully. "How should we handle this? We can hardly go to the chief and say he has vampires on the force. He'll never believe me. We'll have to investigate on our own. And when we find the proof, then what?"

"We'll have to enter their house and hope the boys, at least some of them, are still alive, and then you'll have to find a way to kill the brothers," said Lance, adding, "like you and Will Bradley tried to kill me."

Jack exhaled. "Can we bring Will into this?"

"Isn't he retired?"

"Yes, but I trust him. And Juliette may be able to help. That woman knows everything. She's very resourceful. She can weave a protective spell like nobody's business."

"It will be dangerous," Lance pointed out. He debated whether to tell Jack about the Stryer murders. He had enough information to help Jack close that case. He hated withholding information from his father-in-law, but he knew Zoltan was untouchable. Lance was regaining his strength and his abilities daily, but he wasn't strong enough yet to go up against the count. His final abilities were still an unknown. Would he be as powerful as he once was? Would he be able to transport himself? Would he be a hybrid, half human, half vampire? And what would his child be like? Would he or she be a monster like he was? One thing was certain. In order to defeat Zoltan, he'd have to go back into the fold, and he wasn't going to do that. But he would find a way to get Zoltan out of their lives. He would always be a threat to Aurora Dawn and their child because he would use them to get to Lance, whether by charm or by force.

"I can find out what shift they have tonight and where they live. Then we can pay them a visit, see if the missing boys are there," Jack said.

"And what if they show up while we're there? One of them alone would be formidable. Together they're going to be hard to beat. We have to be prepared to dispatch them." The count's exact words had been "put them down like rabid dogs."

"How would we do that?"

"There are silver bullets. Real bullets made of pure silver. Straight through the heart would do it."

"I've seen those, but aren't they just replicas, not designed to be used in real weapons?"

"I have some real silver bullets, live rounds. Then, of course, there's the wooden or silver stake through the heart, although these guys don't have hearts—or they have black hearts. That's effective, but medieval and gruesome. We could restrain them and let them sizzle in the sunlight, or burn their bodies to ashes, but I wouldn't wish that death on anyone. I've lived through it, and luckily my body was healed, but just barely."

Jack blinked. "I'm not going to apologize for that. You were a threat to my family."

"I was," Lance admitted, "then."

"We're going to have to involve the department,

get a warrant, maybe go in with a strike force, and then if we find the boys and meet with resistance, one of us could shoot them or burn the house down with them in it," Jack said. "Let me get the process started, deal with the paperwork, and round up some guys I can trust. Meanwhile, you can get us some guns that will fire live silver bullets."

"That won't be a problem. I came back from Hungary prepared." Zoltan had given him a suitcase full of every weapon he needed. Lance had taken care of another kind of protection.

"Here," he said, placing a chain with a shining silver cross around Jack's neck. Wear this at all times."

"What about you?"

"I'm immune to them."

"What if we don't get them, and they retaliate? What about Kate and Aurora Dawn?"

Lance handed over a second silver crucifix necklace to Jack. "This is for Kate. Aurora Dawn has the amethyst amulet she wears around her neck, the one her grandmother gave her. No one can harm her as long as she is wearing that. It's a source of goodness and light that serves as a permanent protective barrier. Juliette has her own protective powers, and she will protect Will."

Jack shook Lance's hand. "I appreciate your help. I hope our partnership will become a permanent arrangement. I could use a man like you in my business and, when I'm ready to retire, to take over the business."

Lance returned his father-in-law's strong handshake. Working with Aurora Dawn's father felt right. He had finally found his place, a place where he could do good instead of pursuing a life of leisure and mayhem. He had been drifting through the centuries, untethered, purposeless, and unhappy. He was determined to turn his life around.

"I will do my best for you, sir."

"Welcome to the family, son."

Chapter Thirty-Three

The night was as dark as pitch. The moon illuminated the wooden structure. The Harlan home looked like something out of a horror film—a devil's abode. All it needed to set the stage was some eerie mood music. Evil seemed to shimmer from the unnatural scene and around the edges of the property, along with a thick forest of brambles. Who knew what debauchery had occurred inside? No lights were on, indicating that the brothers weren't in residence, although Jack had already checked the schedule and determined that the twins were on an undercover assignment elsewhere. Right now they weren't after the brothers. They were all about the victims and hoped they weren't on the verge of making a gruesome recovery.

The team was ready to move on Jack's signal.

Jack walked up to the door and knocked loudly. "Tobias and Sebastian Harlan. Open the door. This is the Atlanta Police Department. We have warrants to search this house." No answer.

"Let's break down the door," Jack instructed.

Two APD officers broke down the front door, and the team rushed in.

What they found inside was a chamber of horrors. One young officer puked. The smell of rotting flesh was overwhelming. Jack stared in disbelief. One cop began documenting the scene with his camera.

Jack turned to Lance for an explanation. "Is this… What is this?"

"It's a playground, sir. It's where the brothers take their victims, to dally with or turn or kill."

Lance surveyed the area. It was more like a scene from the Apocalypse. There were two open crypts, beds for the brothers, lined up against the wall. Dead victims in various stages of decomposition were chained to the walls. From out of the darkness came a flapping of wings, and several bat-like creatures dive-bombed the officers and flew out the open door.

"Night creatures feeding on the dead remains," Lance explained to Jack.

"Let's get some ID on what's left of these victims," Jack ordered a young cop. "Check missing persons. These people belonged to someone."

They looked in every room but found no young boys.

Lance led the team down the stairs to the basement. "If they are here, they would likely be held in the basement, away from the noise and the partying. Held in reserve."

Lance knew what Jack was thinking: How would he know? He knew because he had held these orgies himself, held helpless, innocent victims in the basement until it was their turn to party. The memory was still fresh, although it sickened him. He was ashamed, and he knew Jack could read his thoughts.

"If we're lucky, they're still alive, stunned and sedated, but still alive," Lance said. "From the look of things, the vampires and their friends had worked themselves into a blood frenzy of anticipation, but I see no signs that they were—"

The thought of what they might have experienced was so horrific that no words were adequate to describe them.

The team walked one by one into the basement, guns drawn.

Jack turned on the lights and found himself staring into five pairs of frightened eyes. The boys were naked, chained to mattresses on the floor, and must have been kept in the dark for days, judging by the way their eyes were having trouble adjusting to the light.

When they saw the blue uniforms, they began screaming, "They're coming!"

Jack tried to calm the boys. "You're safe now. No one will harm you." It was then he realized what the boys were afraid of. Tobias and Sebastian were cops, therefore also dressed in blue uniforms. He couldn't wait to get his bare hands on those bastards. He could easily kill them.

Jack immediately recognized the boys in the basement. They matched the descriptions of the missing boys who were taken from their beds at night while their parents were home, unaware of the danger that lurked in their midst.

"Get some wire cutters over here," Jack instructed. "Let's get these boys free."

As each victim was cut free, Jack placed a blanket over each of them. "They're exhausted and they're cold. Have you eaten?" Jack asked one of the boys.

He couldn't answer. He was in a daze.

"They were glamoured, sir," Lance said. "They won't remember anything about the abduction. They won't have eaten. The brothers would have wanted them in a weakened condition so they couldn't resist."

"Were they—" Jack couldn't form the words. He cupped his hand around his mouth.

"Doubtful. They would be taken up one at a time to the group, so until then, they would have remained untouched."

"Would they have been—?"

"Anything you can imagine, it would be worse—violated by multiple beings, fed upon, torn apart," answered Lance. "And if they decided to spare a boy, he would be theirs forever. He would be turned into one of them. These boys are lucky. They were spared. But as soon as the brothers came home after their shift, it would have started. The signs are all there."

Jack steadied himself. In all of his cases, in all the years on the force and in private consults, he had never seen anything like this. Serial killers were sickening, but vampires like the Harlan brothers took evil to new heights.

"When are they expected home?" Lance asked.

"Within the hour." Jack instructed the team to take the boys to the station and contact their families.

"We're going to keep a team here to gather DNA evidence."

"You won't find any."

"The team can document what they saw here, and then we'll send them home."

Within the hour, everyone had left the scene but Jack and Lance. They waited outside the house until the Harlan brothers came home.

The twins looked tired but were in good spirits, probably anticipating what they were coming home to.

They looked puzzled when they saw the open front

door, smashed in. Within minutes of entering their house, they let out a series of blood-curdling screams. Somebody had tampered with their lair and taken their treasures.

Lance poured gasoline around the perimeter of the house, starting at the front door, soaking the ground. Jack lit the match. The wooden house went up like a spark. Soon agonizing screams and screeches could be heard throughout the house. Sounds of pounding feet on the floors, flapping wings against the walls. The brothers were trying to escape, through the doors or the windows. But Jack had ordered the team to board up the windows before they left, preventing the brothers from escaping, and the doors were in flames, so now they were trapped. Trapped in a blazing inferno with the house disintegrating around them.

"A straight shot to Hell," Lance observed.

"Should we put them out of their misery?" Jack wondered. "Give them a path out and then shoot them?"

"No," stated Lance. "Let them suffer the way their victims suffered." Smoky memories drifted back to Lance, memories of excruciating pain as the sunlight seared his skin before Zoltan zapped him up out of the bonds of the silver chains on the boat and nurtured him back to life.

"No one can know what happened here," stated Jack, conveying to his son-in-law the illegality of what they had just done, and, at the same time, creating a lasting bond between them.

"They won't hear it from me," Lance promised, knowing he would never be able to erase what he had seen that night.

Chapter Thirty-Four

Eight months later

Lance bit his fingernails. He paced while Aurora Dawn took calming breaths in a hospital room, ready to deliver their child. Was it a boy or a girl? He had said he wanted to be surprised. But what if the boy looked like him? What if the boy *was* like him, a vampire? Well, not a full vampire, but what if he had vampiric tendencies? What if he had a heartless soul? But he would also be the son of Aurora Dawn, so he would get purity and sweetness from his mother.

Or what if it was a girl? A beautiful girl with long golden tresses like Aurora Dawn's but with his black heart? He would love the child, no matter what. Boy or girl, vampire or not, evil or not evil. As long as the baby was healthy, he didn't care. Wasn't that what all normal parents desired for their children?

He'd come to terms with Zoltan. Or pretended to. Zoltan had agreed to stay out of their lives and release Lance from his blood commitment to the Nagy family if he could take one look at the new baby. Just a look. Lance had promised, but he worried that Zoltan was going to try something like the old fairy, in the tale of Sleeping Beauty, who wasn't invited to the christening so she cast an enchantment spell on the princess and her entire household. That was a true tale in vampire lore, by the way, although humans didn't believe it.

To be safe, Zoltan would be invited to the christening to look upon the new baby, after which he had promised to leave them alone. But Zoltan had always been crafty, so Lance and Jack had a plan to capture his Maker. He should go to prison for the Stryer murders but no jail could hold him. Lance would shoot him straight through the heart with one of the silver bullets still stored in the weapon Zoltan had provided. It was the only way to keep his family safe. It would be the last crime he would commit.

"Lance," cried Aurora Dawn. "Hurry." She must be in distress. He hurried in, just in time to see his daughter's head crowning, and he witnessed her birth. No signs of the Devil. Just a beautiful head of yellow curls.

The nurse put the baby into his hands and left the room. He cradled her in his arms. She was pure beauty and light. An angel. He was sure she didn't have a drop of his blood or a trace of his evil. At least he hoped not. Five fingers on each hand and five toes. No marks. Two beautifully shaped eyebrows.

He placed the baby into Aurora Dawn's arms. "Your daughter is perfect."

"Our daughter," Aurora Dawn corrected. "And no one is perfect. For all we know, she's going to grow up to be a little imp."

"Don't even think that," Lance cautioned.

Aurora Dawn kissed each of the baby's cheeks. "Look, Lance, she has your green eyes."

Lance looked closer. "You think so?"

"Absolutely."

Lance smiled broadly.

The nurse reentered the room. "I think the baby's grandparents and great-grandparents want a look."

For a minute, Lance imagined that Gwenn and Art, his pseudo parents, might make an unwanted appearance. He had been happy to see the last of them.

Thankfully, it was Kate and Jack, with Juliette and Will, who bustled in.

"Oh, my," said Kate. "She's a beauty. She looks just like Aurora Dawn when she was a baby. Except Aurora Dawn had black ringlets before her hair turned blonde. And Lance, she has your eyes."

"I know," said Lance proudly.

"I come bearing gifts," said Juliette. She drew out a tiny amethyst amulet from her handbag and placed it around the baby's neck. It slid to the side and nestled into the blanket.

"It's been blessed," assured Juliette. "No harm can come to her as long as she wears this amulet."

Lance breathed a sigh of relief. Zoltan had strong powers, but Juliette was a force to be reckoned with. In fact, all of the women in Aurora Dawn's family were. Zoltan could cast his eyes on their child, but he would be powerless against Juliette's magic and Aurora Dawn's fierce maternal protectiveness. Lance's powers were growing exponentially. One day soon, he would surpass Zoltan. He would protect his family from any harm.

"Have you thought of a name, sweetheart?" Jack asked his daughter.

"Well, we haven't talked about names," Lance began.

"Yes," Aurora Dawn answered. "We're going to call the baby Marika."

Lance choked and suddenly teared up. "Aurora Dawn—"

"After an old childhood friend of Lance's who was very important to him."

"What a lovely name," Kate said.

"It's a very powerful name," agreed Juliette. "Marika was the matriarch of our family."

Lance looked at Aurora Dawn and didn't think he could love her any more than he did at that moment. He was amazed that she would place so much trust in him as to name their baby after his first love. He put his finger up to Marika's tiny hand, and the infant wound it tightly around him. She had a powerful grip. She already owned his heart.

"Marika Gigi Lakeland," said Aurora Dawn, taking the baby's middle name from Gedeon. Gigi was the name they'd discussed, Gigi for Gedeon, so the child would always have a piece of her father's heritage.

"Gigi, that's the name of the heroine in your new vampire novel, isn't it?" Kate asked. "The woman who won the vampire's heart and turned him from his evil ways? Saved him from himself?"

"Yes, because he was essentially good. And I have a publication date for the book. It's coming out in time for the new year."

"Second chances," whispered Lance.

"Second chances," nodded Aurora Dawn, as she cuddled their child between them and beamed a pure look of profound love at her husband.

Epilogue

"I can't say I like what you've done to the place," Zoltan said. "A little too prissy for my taste. Especially the nursery. What style is this? Early sweetness and light? And what was wrong with fuschia? I can't abide by that heavenly blue your wife had the exterior painted."

"I gave Aurora Dawn and her mother carte blanche on redecorating. Nothing is too good for my wonderful wife and our little angel," Lance beamed proudly, looking down at Marika fast asleep in her crib.

"She is spectacular," agreed Zoltan.

Lance frowned.

"And speaking of spectacular, where is your lovely wife tonight?"

"Next door, visiting her mother." He would never allow Zoltan to be in the same room with his wife again.

"A pity. Well, give her my regards."

Zoltan approached the crib where the infant was sleeping. He reached out his hand.

Lance's right hand fisted and he stopped his former Maker from touching Marika.

"She's sleeping and I don't want to disturb her."

"At least tell me what color her eyes are."

"They're green, like mine," Lance said, allowing himself a moment of pride. "Zoltan, that's one of the reasons I invited you here. You've seen her. Now it's time for you to go. That was our agreement."

"No matter. I can come back and see my grandchild when she's awake."

Lance exhaled. "Marika is no relation to you. And you won't be coming back."

"And how are you going to stop me?"

Lance flexed his muscles. "I know you've been attempting to invade our dreams, mine and Aurora Dawn's.

Zoltan laughed. "I have to do something to pass the time."

"Why don't we go downstairs to the keeping room and have a celebratory drink."

"You know I don't drink."

"Well, then you can watch while I drink."

"Very well. Race you down." Zoltan flew down the stairs while Lance covered Marika with a light blanket to ward off the chill in the air. He took the stairs slowly, trying to regain his composure. He could have flown. He chose not to. He didn't want to reveal his growing strength and powers to Zoltan.

When they were both in the keeping room, Jack appeared out of the shadows.

"I've taken the liberty of inviting my father-in-law to have a drink with us."

Zoltan turned to Jack and extended his hand. "I am Zoltan. I'm sure Gedeon has told you all about me."

"*Lance* has filled me in on your history," said Jack, who moved closer to Zoltan, but refused the offer of friendship.

Lance approached from behind and twisted Zoltan's hands behind his back. Zoltan tried to escape but Lance's hands bound him like steel ropes.

"So, the pupil has surpassed the master."

Lance remained silent while Jack quickly cuffed the vampire with silver manacles. Zoltan sprang back in pain.

"Zoltan Nagy, you are under arrest for the murders of the Stryer family. You have the right to remain silent—" Jack began.

"Don't bother reading me my rights. No jail can hold me. You're wasting your time." Zoltan strained against the handcuffs.

"You agreed to one look and then you would leave my family alone," said Lance.

"One look will never be enough."

Lance casually opened a drawer at the bar and removed a hand gun, the gun Zoltan had provided him. The gun with the silver bullets. He came around to face Zoltan.

Zoltan forced a smile. "You would never kill me. You love me."

"I don't want to do this," Lance said. "But you leave me no choice."

"Think of what we have meant to each other."

"My family is the only thing that's important to me now."

"I am your family," Zoltan cried.

Lance raised the pistol and aimed for Zoltan's heart.

Jack didn't hesitate. He ran to Lance and grabbed the gun from his son-in-law's shaking hands. He pushed Lance aside, took aim and the bullet found its target.

An ungodly scream echoed across the room. Then

Zoltan disappeared in a flash of lightning, a crack of thunder and the burn of an angry hiss. The only thing that remained in his place were the silver handcuffs. It was a miracle that the commotion didn't awaken Marika.

Lance flinched and his hand flew to his heart.

"He's gone forever," Jack said.

"Why did you do that? I just wanted to scare him into leaving us alone."

"Lance, you couldn't see it. He was never going to go. He deserved to be punished for what he did to the Stryer family and what he would surely continue to do to threaten yours."

"I've done worse," Lance objected, rubbing his hands across his face. "I should have been the one to take his life."

"I could see you were struggling. You're a good man, Lance, and I didn't want his death on your conscience, son."

Lance's eyes threatened to tear up at that term of endearment. He was finally being accepted by Aurora Dawn's father as a real member of the family. Jack grasped his son-in-law's shoulder in solidarity.

"I'm glad it's done," Lance admitted.

"That makes two of us," Jack said. "Now, let's have that drink before Aurora Dawn gets home or my granddaughter wakes up. We have a lot to celebrate."

A word about the author...

Marilyn Baron writes humorous coming-of-*middle-age* women's fiction, historical romantic thrillers, suspense, and paranormal/fantasy. A public relations consultant in Atlanta, she's a PAN member of Romance Writers of America (RWA) and Georgia Romance Writers (GRW) and winner of the GRW 2009 Chapter Service Award and writing awards in single title, suspense romance, paranormal/fantasy, and novel with strong romantic elements. She's also a member of the 2016-17 Roswell Reads Committee.

She graduated from the University of Florida in Gainesville, Florida, with a Bachelor of Science in Journalism (Public Relations sequence) and a minor in Creative Writing. Born in Miami, Florida, Marilyn lives in Roswell, GA, with her husband, and they have two daughters.

To find out more about Marilyn's books, please visit her Web site at www.marilynbaron.com.